ERICA LAINÉ was born in South
nally studied for the theatre at th
in Tring. She worked as a librar
trained as a speech and drama te
her family to Hong Kong in 1977
British Council for twenty years as a teacher and educational
project manager.

Since 1997 she has lived in south-west France where she
became interested in all sorts of historical research and writing, as President of the Aquitaine Historical Society. This led
to a focus on Isabella of Angoulême and her life and times.
The Aquitaine region is rich in English and French history
and Isabella is a person who was woven into both. Erica
has begun writing part two of The Tangled Queen which
will show how Isabella played all sides against each other
and how her intrigues became part of the beginning of the
Hundred Years' War.

Isabella OF Angoulême

ERICA LAINÉ

SilverWood

Published in 2015 by SilverWood Books

SilverWood Books Ltd
14 Small Street, Bristol, BS1 1DE, United Kingdom
www.silverwoodbooks.co.uk

ISBN 978-1-78132-457-8 (paperback)
ISBN 978-1-78132-458-5 (ebook)

British Library Cataloguing in Publication Data
A CIP catalogue record for this book is available from
the British Library

Set in Sabon by SilverWood Books
Printed on responsibly sourced paper

Dedicated to JRL

FRANCE 1200
PLANTAGENET POSSESSIONS

Anjou, Maine – inherited by Henry
    I through Geoffrey of Anjou and
    Queen Matilda of England
Normandy – taken and controlled by
    Henry I 1120
Aquitaine, Gascony – lands gained by
    Henry II's marriage to Eleanor of
    Aquitaine
Brittany – land gained by his son
    Geoffrey's marriage to Constance of
    Brittany
**Blois, Burgundy, Champagne, Flanders,
    Toulouse** – lands which recognised
    the French king as overlord

HOUSE OF CAPET

CAPETIAN HOUSE OF COURTNEY

Louis VI of France m(2) Adelaide de Maurienne

Philippe
d1131

Louis VII m Eleanor of Aquitaine
(div 1152)

Peter of France m Elizabeth, Lady de Courtney

Peter de Courtney,
Latin Emperor
of Constantinople

Alice de Courtney m(1) Guillaume, Count de Joigny (div 1186)

Peter de Joigny
born before 1184

Ademar Taillefer (2) 1186

HOUSE OF TAILLEFER – COUNTS OF ANGOULÊME

William VI m Marguerite du Turrene

William VII

Isabella of Angoulême m(1) 1200 John, King of England
b 1188   m(2) 1220 Hugh X of Lusignan

Wulgin III

Mathilde m ————— Hugh IX of Lusignan   (betrothed 1199)

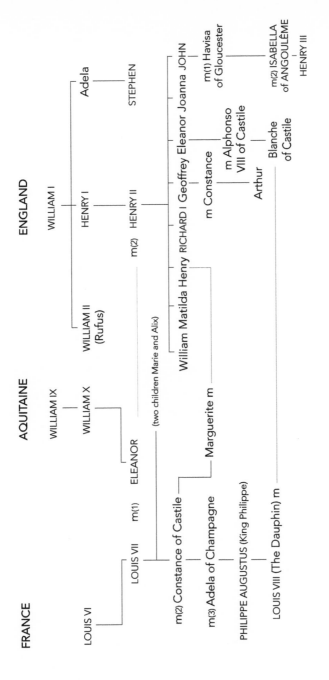

FRANCE

LOUIS VI

LOUIS VII   m(1)   ELEANOR

m(2) Constance of Castile

m(3) Adela of Champagne

PHILIPPE AUGUSTUS (King Philippe)

LOUIS VIII (The Dauphin) m

(two children Marie and Alix)

Marguerite m

AQUITAINE

WILLIAM IX

WILLIAM X

ENGLAND

WILLIAM I

WILLIAM II
(Rufus)

HENRY I

Adela

STEPHEN

m(2) HENRY II

William Matilda Henry RICHARD I Geoffrey Eleanor Joanna JOHN

m Constance

m Alphonso
VIII of Castile

Arthur

Blanche
of Castile

m(1) Havisa
of Gloucester

m(2) ISABELLA
of ANGOULÊME

HENRY III

Characters

Joan – Queen of Scotland, born 1210.

Isabelle – born 1214, married to Frederick II Holy Roman Emperor.

Eleanor – born 1215 married to William Marshall second Earl of Pembroke and then to Simon de Montfort 6th Earl of Leicester.

The English Court

William Marshall – First Earl of Pembroke, the chief Justicar.

The House of Capet

Louis VI the fat.

Louis VII the young – son of Louis VI, married to Eleanor of Aquitaine, divorced 1152.

Philip II Augustus – his son by his third wife.

Louis VIII – Philip II's son married to Blanche of Castile.

Blanche of Castile – his wife, the granddaughter of Eleanor of Aquitaine and John's niece.

The House of Lusignan

Hugh IX of Lusignan – betrothed to Isabella of Angoulême, married Matilda, Ademar's niece after 1200.

Ralph of Eu – his brother.

Hugh X of Lusignan – Hugh's son by his first wife, married to Isabella of Angoulême in 1220.

Poitevin Counts

Aimery, Viscount of Thouars.

Guy of Thouars.

William des Roches, Seneschal of Anjou.

The House of Angoulême

Ademar of Angoulême – Count of Angoulême.

Alice de Courtenay – his wife, granddaughter of Louis VI.

Isabella – their daughter, heiress to Angoulême in her own right, born circa 1189 married to King John August 24 1200. Married Hugh X of Lusignan in 1220.

Peter de Joigny – Alice's son by her first marriage, Isabella's half brother.

Courtiers

Agnes Roussie – Isabella's maid and lady in waiting.
Oliver Bonneville – young knight of Angoulême.
Geoffroy Bonneville – young knight of Angoulême.

The House of Limoges

Guy – Viscount of Limoges.

The Church

Pope Innocent III – a powerful and influential Pope, 1198–1216.
Hubert Walter – Archbishop of Canterbury 1193–1205.
Stephen Langton – Archbishop of Canterbury 1207–1228.
Peter des Roches – Bishop of Winchester and later Justicar and Guardian/Regent to Henry III.

Anglo French Barons

Hubert de Burgh.
William de Briouze.
Peter de Mauley.
Hugh de Neville.
Robert Fitzwalter.

Introduction

The Plantagenet dynasty ruled from 1154 to 1485 and their lands stretched from the borders with Scotland to the Pyrenees. The word empire was not one used during their time. The 12th century Count of Anjou had worn a sprig of broom or genet as a symbol and this brought about the name Plantagenets, but in France they were also known as Angevins, because of their fiefdom or county of Anjou. They won control of a vast area that included Maine and Touraine and then, very importantly, Normandy.

Normandy had been given to the original Norsemen or Vikings in 911 by the French king. William the Conqueror joined Normandy and England together on his 1066 conquest and the whole Anglo-Norman, Anglo-French tangle began.

Henry II inherited the English throne and these lands in France as the son of Geoffrey of Anjou and Queen Matilda. She was the granddaughter of William the Conqueror, so when Henry married Eleanor of Aquitaine this brought together a huge territory. The French kings at this time had very little royal territory as France was made up of several areas which regarded themselves as autonomous.

The medieval Aquitaine that was Eleanor's was huge, the greater part of France, but the borders fluctuated. The people who lived there were very independent and did not care much for any authority except their feudal lord. Isabella of Angoulême was of the Taillefer family who had beaten back the Vikings in the 9th century. The town and its surroundings were always a vital crossroads. Lusignan was a neighbouring fiefdom; the county of La Marche and the Limousin were close by. The families of these places intermarried and quarrelled for several generations. All were land hungry.

In The Tangled Queen the people from this area are referred to as Poitevins rather than Aquitanians or Angoumoisins.

Modern Aquitaine as from 2016 will consist of three regions; Aquitaine, Limousin and Poitou-Charente. It is now closer to the old Aquitaine in size and extent. It will be the largest region in France, about the same size as Austria.

I

Lusignan, June 1200

'Isabella? Isabella, where are you? You are wanted in the great hall. They will be back from hunting very soon.'

Agnes grumbled and muttered as she searched the rooms where Isabella was supposed to be, and, not finding her, went out into the herb garden. Isabella was wandering about, picking lavender sprigs.

'In God's Heaven, child, what are you doing out here? I must dress you for the feast, make you look your best. Hugh of Lusignan must show the new English king that his bride is beautiful as well as an important heiress.'

Isabella jumped onto a low stone wall that edged the garden and shouted at Agnes. 'When I am finally married to Hugh, when I finally become a woman, when I finally help to rule this territory, this fiefdom, I will be Countess of Lusignan, Countess of Angoulême and Lady of La Marche. Say those titles after me, Agnes. Will I not be of great importance? More important than anyone else between Poitiers and Bordeaux.'

Agnes was frequently exasperated with Isabella. Beautiful she might have been, but her wilful ways were not helpful. The twelve-year-old girl seemed to think she could do as she pleased, and that was not what a lord and his castle would

17

want. Isabella was young, true, but she had to learn many skills and manners so that she could take her place beside her husband.

But Isabella often behaved badly, exclaiming how she found the days very tedious, and showing this by either working very slowly indeed, endlessly sighing over her work, or racing through it in a slapdash manner that meant stitches had to be unpicked time and time again, that wool had to be unwound and ledgers laboriously corrected. She had been scolded so often for wanting to escape the embroidery, the weaving and the arithmetic.

Agnes – only five years older than Isabella but still her lady-in-waiting, her companion from home, bossy and benevolent – repeated the constant refrain again now. 'You will need to know how to behave in company – it is not just a matter of gaining titles. You need to know how to sew and weave, to order goods, to keep a check on trade. To help manage the castle and domain with Hugh, and even more importantly, without him. What if he goes away again on a crusade? You have to know how to ready the castle in case of siege.' She tugged Isabella down from the wall and pinched her arm as she hurried her back to the castle.

'Did you see them this morning when they went to the forest to hunt?' Isabella squirmed away from Agnes and ran ahead of her. 'I did – the Lusignans are great huntsmen. And young Hugh, my Lord of Lusignan's son, went with them today – he spends all his time near the stables. I saw them all.'

The hunting party had set off early, the dogs excited and baying, huntsmen blowing horns. Shouts and orders filled the air. Isabella knew that the Lusignans were rightly very proud of their hunting skills. The founder of their dynasty had been the chief huntsman to the Count of Poitou, and a huntsman always appeared on their shields. The memory of this lived on as the hunting party streamed out of the well-guarded gateway – the pack of noisy hounds, eager horses, men already riding hard in the clear July morning. They disappeared down into the forest, a bright river of movement swallowed up by the dark green.

Lusignan had been built on a natural strongpoint: a narrow promontory that overlooked steep valleys on either side. There were strong outer walls and a sturdy tower above the main gate. First a village and then a town had grown up beneath the castle. It was an impressive place, and strategically important in the heart of southwest France.

Raymondin, the marcher lord, had chosen well when he built this great castle two hundred years before. Everyone marvelled at how strong it was, and how beautiful, and how quickly it had been built.

Isabella wondered about this too as she half-ran, half-walked into her chamber set within the thick stone walls, with Agnes at her heels, both of them breathless.

Agnes helped her pull her gown over her head and then stripped off her linen chemise. A wooden tub of hot water, scented with thyme and myrtle oil, was ready and Isabella climbed in. Agnes soaped her back and threw jugs of water over her head. Isabella gazed up at the canopy above the tub, dreaming of power.

'What a kingdom John has inherited!'

'From the Scottish borders to the Pyrenees,' said Agnes. 'It's a good job his mother is still alive to help him keep it.'

Isabella wriggled her toes in the warm water. She knew that Eleanor had been the wife of both a French king and an English king. 'His mother, Eleanor? She's in Fontevraud Abbey, isn't she?'

'Yes,' said Agnes, 'back from Castile and making sure her granddaughter Blanche marries a French king, or a king-to-be. She never stops watching out for her family.' Agnes turned to the fire and grabbed some cloths to dry Isabella.

'Out now, and be quick – I must get you dry and dressed.'

Isabella climbed out and allowed herself to be bundled into the cloths and rubbed dry. A new creamy white chemise was brought and slipped over her head, and next the green and gold silk brocade overtunic was settled over that. This wide pleated skirt and tight bodice with its trailing trumpet sleeves was the first of many new gowns that had been made for her betrothal.

Isabella pulled at the sleeves, shaking them over her wrists as they swept to the floor. Agnes wound a girdle around her waist and knotted it at the front, silky tassels falling softly over the brocade. Small, light brocade shoes were brought, and then Agnes combed her hair straight and glossy.

'My guirland,' ordered Isabella, and waved towards a chest in the corner of the room.

Agnes placed the fine gold filigree band of flowers on her head and declared Isabella ready for the great hall.

She had been summoned to wait for the hunting party to return. The messengers had arrived earlier that week, announcing that the new English king was making a progress through Aquitaine, on his way to Portugal and a possible new bride. Now the Lusignan lords, Hugh and Ralph, were out hunting in the forest with King John and Isabella had been told to greet them when they came in.

Isabella walked around the trestle tables that were laden with food and wine for the feast to come. She nibbled little marzipan hedgehogs studded with almonds, and stole some strawberries dipped in wine. A large pewter dish of suckling pig stood proud in the centre, surrounded by plates of chickens stuffed with parsley, and smaller ones full of quails roasted with garlic and ginger, and river trout steamed with young onions. Tureens and bowls were being brought in, and servants bustled about finding room for yet another platter.

She moved away from the table and towards the far end of the great hall, away from the door which would soon burst open with men, dogs, noise and clamour. Her Lord of Lusignan, Hugh, would be there with his brother Ralph, Hugh pleased with his new title, Lord of La Marche, and the fiefdom that went with it. A gift from the new king.

Isabella wanted to think about that: meeting a king for the first time.

She had tried to catch a glimpse of him when his travelling group swept up to the gates of the castle at Lusignan the day before, but had been hurried away by Agnes, and scolded for neglecting her work. But the day passed quickly as the women laughed and gossiped. The stories of magical help from Melusine were told to Isabella as she learnt to spin and weave. The stories were whispered and woven into the tapestries, with silky dragonflies and serpents to bear witness forever.

Isabella remembered them now as she waited in the great hall, her fingers tracing the patterns in the tapestries hanging on the wall – some rich and dark, others glowing with bright silks.

As they had worked, Joan, an old nursemaid, told them the story, as it had been told and retold to women in the weaving room forever. Her voice was soft and sibilant, her hands stroking the woven cloth that lay across her lap.

'Melusine was a water spirit, born to a fairy who had loved a king of the northern lands. Melusine was full of wise magic, and left her mother's house to live in the forest of Colombiers.'

Isabella listened carefully. Colombiers was nearby, full of streams and bogs, a perfect place for a water spirit to choose.

'One twilight evening, while she and some of her fairy court were guarding the Fountain of Thirst, their sacred fountain, a young man, Raymondin of Poitiers, stumbled upon them. He

21

was lost and troubled after a hunting accident that had killed his uncle.'

'Accident?' snorted Agnes. 'Murder, more likely.'

Joan lifted one hand and Agnes bit her lip and stopped.

'Melusine spent the night soothing and consoling Raymondin, and by dawn, had helped him conceal his uncle's body. He gazed at her with longing, for he found her beauty so enchanting, so desirable, that he wanted her with him always. And so they married, but there was one condition. Melusine made Raymondin promise that he would never enter her bedchamber or bathing place on a Saturday.'

The women who wove the story into their work agreed that there was often a hard and fatal condition attached to any pairing of fairy and mortal.

'Raymondin promised that he would obey, and Melusine brought her husband great wealth and prosperity. She built the fortress of Lusignan so quickly that it appeared to have been made by magic. They say she only needed to use two handfuls of stones and a mouthful of water. And there was the castle! A place for peace and prosperity, a place where they could have a family. Indeed, they had many children, but all with some strange flaw. Despite this, they were loved and cherished anyway.'

Isabella had stopped spinning and was sitting still and quiet as the story unfolded.

'Now Raymondin became very suspicious about his wife. So one Saturday, he spied on her through the door of her chamber. What horror! He saw that she was half-woman and half-serpent. But he did not tell her that he had seen her, and all was harmony. Then one day, in anger, Raymondin called Melusine a serpent in front of everyone gathered in the great hall. Lusignan's great hall.'

'What did she do?'

'She wailed and cried like the cold north wind – oh,

pitiful to hear – and then she changed into a great, green dragon-serpent, circling the castle three times and lamenting for her children. She flew away, returning at night to visit them but always vanishing before dawn. Now it is said that she appears at the castle whenever a Count of Lusignan is about to die, or a new one to be born.'

Later, as they chose new wool Isabella had asked Agnes, 'Will Melusine come when I give birth to a new count?'

Agnes had laughed, pinched her cheek and told her not to think about babies just yet, and to get on with her spinning.

As Isabella traced the patterns she thought about the magic that had captured Raymondin, and how he had betrayed his wife and children. I would be a dragon too if my husband betrayed me, she thought fiercely, and she stood a little taller and felt a stirring of anger at the thought of love and its betrayal.

A commotion at the door of the great hall made her turn quickly. Was the hunt home? A man appeared at the door: short and stocky, with brownish-red hair. It was true, then, that the youngest son of the great Henry II and Eleanor of Aquitaine was also the shortest. Nicknamed Lackland by his father at his birth, he also lacked height. But then there was the thrilling realisation that this was the new king. King John looked about him – angry, pleased and searching for something, all at the same time. Isabella watched carefully, noticing the anger more than anything else. John began eating, devouring pieces of the suckling pig, noisily swallowing beakers of the local red wine, tearing at bread, and then he turned back towards the door.

'Well, Hugh, where is this bride of yours, the girl who makes you feel such a lord?'

Hugh Lusignan, taller and darker than John, strode purposefully into the hall, rubbing his hands together and whistling to his two favourite hunting dogs. He reached for the garlic-stuffed quail, throwing bits to the dogs, and wiped greasy hands before he spoke.

'Isabella? She is in here – she was sent for.' And he looked towards the dark end of the great hall. 'Isabella.'

The command was firm. Slowly she walked forward, her dark green silk dress pooling around her feet and the candle-light making glints in her long hair. Hugh fixed his eyes upon her as she walked into the light. She raised hers to acknowl-edge him, and was glad to see Hugh le Brun, tall and dark, the Lord of Lusignan.

'Isabella of Angoulême.' A proud declaration from Hugh.

'My lord.' An answer to whom? She felt sure that her reply was to both men, as she bowed and inclined her head, and swept a curtsey, low and demure.

Hugh spoke again, impatient now. 'My liege, this is Isabella. We have been betrothed for over a year, we have exchanged binding vows and will marry soon, when the time is ripe – all very straightforward. She is heiress to Angoulême in her own right, and the marriage will cement the Lusignan and Angoumois lands. This should stop trouble fermenting and keep King Philippe away.'

John lifted a hand as if to swat a fly, and then pulled Isabella upright, tilting her head by her chin. She stared into dark, fierce eyes, again sensing the anger that seemed to lie at the heart of his every gesture.

He saw a young girl, admired for her beauty throughout France. She had inherited a strong line from her mother Alice, granddaughter of Louis VI, and her slender figure showed the promise of a full womanhood. Her face was serene, full-lipped, dark-browed and with the long, tawny hair of the Taillefer family, who had held positions of power since Charlemagne. And her eyes – a mix of green and hazel – were full of mischief, pride and a certain wilfulness.

John let go of her chin, smiled at Hugh and turned his attention to a dish of hot vegetables dressed with oil and butter. His beard was messy with food. A servant offered a bowl of hot water and a linen cloth and he scrubbed his face.

'A bath, I think, after such a heavy day's hunting. Does your watery ancestor still wash herself in this place?'

Hugh gave a short bark of a laugh and threw an arm around a third man who had just come in from the hunt. 'Well, Ralph, do we still expect to see serpents in the bedchambers?'

His brother smiled and murmured, 'No, Hugh, we seem to have given up on that.'

King John began to leave the great hall, calling servants to him and shouting orders for hot water, but glanced over at Isabella, who was standing quiet and still, her hands folded in front of her.

'And you, Isabella of Angoulême – what did you do today while we hunted deer in the forest?'

'I sewed, my lord.'

'A fine seam?'

'I hope so, my lord.'

'Tomorrow I shall look at your fine seams and see if they are straight and true.'

Isabella dipped her chin. 'My lord.'

And then he was gone, and Hugh walked her back to the entrance where he called for Agnes to accompany her to her chamber, said a long, serious goodnight, full of praise for her demeanour, and gave a promise that he too would see her sewing in the morning, before returning the great hall where he would talk over the day with Ralph.

Isabella trailed in front of Agnes up the stone steps to her room, and when she was wrapped in her nightclothes she stood in the recess by the small arched window where a thick curtain kept out the drafts. She thought about the king she had just met, and decided that she did not like him at all. He was exciting in a dangerous way, but there was too much cruelty in those eyes.

She wondered how Hugh and Ralph would keep on his good side, she wondered how long he would be king, and she wondered about the visit the following day when he would see her at work with needle and thread.

Sighing, she climbed into bed, glad of the covers despite the warm summer's night. Something cold had crept into Lusignan.

II

Lusignan and Angoulême, June 1200

The morning was bright and clear, and after prayers the women gathered in the sewing room, Isabella working on the seams for a chemise. This was fine, fiddly work as the seam had to be invisible when finished. She had already unpicked it twice and now, bent over her needle, knew that this piece of sewing was not going to be any better. She could feel the impatience rising within her, an indigestible lump that made it hard to swallow. She hated sewing intensely, and longed to throw the half-finished garment onto the floor and run out of the room.

At this point John, Hugh and Ralph entered, whistling and calling to two spaniels that Ralph had brought with him from Normandy. They were eager hunting dogs but small and friendly, so good companions too.

Isabella stood, as did all the other women, and curtseyed. John plucked the sewing from her hands and pretended to examine it. He threw it across to Hugh with a laugh.

'Your bride will not make her fortune sewing,' he said. 'What would you rather be doing on this fine, bright day?

'Hunting, my lord. Walking in the forest, picking strawberries, planting herbs, writing accounts, drying lavender – anything but this,' she burst out.

John laughed again. 'I think some hunting could be arranged. These two dogs need a lesson, do they not, Ralph?'

'Indeed they do.'

'Well then, let Isabella take them into the forest and see what they can find.'

And with that, he was out of the room and down the stairs.

There was a murmur from all around the room as the women began to move about, packing away thread and fabric. Isabella looked at Hugh with a questioning expression – would she be allowed to go out?

'You may take the spaniels and a pony for a walk in the forest, but not on your own. Let my son accompany you – he can begin to train the dogs.'

Isabella and young Hugh trotted through the trees, with the spaniels running about ahead. The dogs soon found the scent of rabbits and were off, barking furiously. Isabella spurred her horse on, while Hugh shouted at the dogs to wait. They paid no attention and rushed into a small copse where there was a warren. Hugh dismounted and strode in, breaking a switch from a tree as he went and swearing.

'God's teeth, this is not what is wanted. They need to be taken out on foot to begin with – this is madness to ride with them.'

Isabella rode on a little. She wanted to enjoy the ride, and the forest and the freedom. It wasn't really hunting, but it was glorious to be away from the usual routine. Her pony suddenly stopped, spooked by a shadow, and out of the shadow came King John.

'My lord,' Isabella said at once.

'Isabella, shall we ride?'

He reached forward and took hold of her reins, leading her pony towards his horse until he could touch her. With one hand holding the reins he stroked her face with the other, touching her lips with his fingers and then lingering on her throat. Then he laughed, and gave her back her reins.

'Your father arrives tomorrow from Angoulême. I shall tell him what a beautiful daughter he has.'

He turned towards Lusignan and disappeared. Hugh shouted something at the spaniels – 'Come here! Stay! Wait!' – and the rapturous trance was broken.

Together with the dogs they slowly made their way back to the Château. Hugh took charge of the ponies and disappeared to the stables. Isabella made her way to her chamber and sat for a long time, thinking and wondering. She felt fearful. She knew that Hugh, Lord of La Marche, was to marry her and was waiting for her, but he had never looked at her or touched her as she had been looked at and touched by the king. Was this what a king's love meant: to be half-trembling for hours after the meeting, to have thoughts that disturbed her very soul? She knelt by her bed and prayed with more meaning than she had ever felt before.

Thirty leagues away in Angoulême, the triple bells rang for the angelus. It was six in the morning and clear all the way to the river. Ademar and Alice stood at the window of their bedchamber, looking down and out across the town of Angoulême that huddled around the castle. Built on a rocky outcrop, it dominated the Charente as it flowed so strongly, with its often-flooded banks and water meadows.

Here on the steep hill the castle and the town were safe as they always had been since the first count had built his castle nearly four hundred years earlier. And the thick, strong ramparts, the strong fortifications that had been started two centuries ago and which Ademar was strengthening, provided even more protection against attack. The town was wealthy, with a fine cathedral and a bishop's palace. The Angoumois people were proud of their prosperity and Ademar had a land-hunger, a glorying in ownership, a need to jealously guard what was his and theirs that everyone understood. Lusignan would be joined to Angoulême, La Marche would come to Angoulême, and the three counties would make up a great fiefdom.

'Isabella is too young for the marriage bed,' Isabella's mother, Alice de Courtney, said. 'She may look beautiful but she has not yet started her flux, and it is considered more fortunate to wait for that before we strew the chamber with rose petals.'

Ademar agreed that this was sound, honest advice, and besides, it was canon law.

'You must ask her maid if she has had need of monthly bandages,' Alice said as she helped him fasten his wide leather belt.

'I would prefer you to have that conversation. Come with me to visit her, Alice. Mothers are more necessary than fathers at these times.'

'It is not a visit, it is a summons from John to pay him homage, to swear fealty. A necessary recognition, as the king, my cousin, tells us only too clearly.'

Alice was the granddaughter of one late King of France, cousin to another, influential in her own right and together she and Ademar had bred a daughter who possessed the same powerful mix of pride and ambition.

Ademar was a true heir to the Taillefer legacy of fierce fighters, those men who had been put in place by Charlemagne to hold off the Viking raids when the longboats prowled the coasts of Europe and sailed up the rivers, searching for treasure and land. His loyalty was to his fiefdom and his family. He scorned the kings in Paris and London – they were too far away to cause him trouble. He liked his own way. He sat heavily on a stool by the window and revisited the memory of the revolt against Richard, a revolt that Ademar had led. Richard had constantly harried the Poitevin counts, and eventually subdued them all. Ademar swore a most reluctant allegiance at the time of bitter surrender. Richard's death had found him allied to Philippe, the French king who was desperate to drive the English out of France.

'I have come to an agreement with him on such terms that I will help him to the best of my ability,' Ademar had reported. 'He has promised us La Marche in return.'

And then John had become king, giving out titles and territory to all who supported him, and the Lusignans had won La Marche from him. Ademar, thwarted, furious, but cunning, had seen the need to reconcile with the counts of Lusignan. And God's blood, Angoulême's pride needed to be restored!

He stood and began to pace. Isabella was a useful daughter – beautiful, too. That she was precocious he knew, but he didn't care about that. Hugh le Brun would have to deal with her, and when Isabella became pregnant and gave birth it would help to calm her down, or so Alice said. As he turned about the room, his steps echoed his thoughts. Binding personal vows. They had been taken. A good preparation for the nuptial benediction. An important betrothal; the marriage even more so. A marriage to be celebrated, and soon, despite Isabella's age.

'Was it true that Hugh Lusignan captured Eleanor on her way to Spain and held her until she promised him La Marche?' asked Alice. She had been furious that La Marche had fallen from their grasp, her proud claims dashed.

'That is what is said by some. It could be true, but I thought she was too wily for such tactics. She made that great tour of her duchy to ensure it all stayed loyal to her and to John. John is not a man to win land for himself if there is any resistance. She even paid homage to Philippe for her own lands of Poitou and Aquitaine, but that was a wise move – it blocked Arthur of Brittany's claim.'

'And John is newly divorced – a wife put aside as soon as he becomes king.'

'She proved to be barren after ten years of trying, but John has many bastards. No lack there!'

'And now he travels south to Portugal, hoping to form a marriage alliance with a daughter of the Portuguese king – well, his brother married a Spanish bride. Berengaria waits to see who will pay her widow's dowry. John is ever reluctant.'

Alice was sealing a letter to Isabella. It had been so long since they had met and spoken, but this was the way it worked: once betrothed to Hugh of Lusignan, Isabella must reside in his castle and be taught all the skills of a chatelaine. Alice had written about the importance of the marriage, reminding Isabella once more:

> *It will be a marriage that will end the discord between our two families, a discord that has disrupted this region for too long.*

Ademar took the letter, and Alice held his hand and whispered, 'Give it to her with my blessing.'

Ademar kissed her bowed head. She must be missing Isabella more than he recognised. The place was certainly quieter without her and her maids, Isabella's imperious voice commanding them to play. Blind Man's Bluff was a favourite, and shrieks and mocking laughter had echoed through the rooms. She had other maids about her now – only her oldest, Agnes Roussie, had gone with Isabella to help ease her into her new life.

Alice walked with him to the yard where the horses and men waited. Ademar had flung a cloak of fine claret-red wool over his browny-gold tunic. A young horseman carried the red and gold chequered flag of Angoulême, and all present had touches of red and gold about them. As the sun rose higher it lit up the colours of defiance and wealth.

Now they must ride to Lusignan, where Ademar would meet King John. John had called on Ademar to swear fealty in a place where he was among friends. Ademar tensed his hands on the reins as he thought of this, and as he rode hard across the rocky land that linked his stronghold of Angoulême and Lusignan. A close, tough knot of men rode with him and behind him. It was a hot day and the sun was warm on their backs as they travelled west. Wheat was ripening fast in the small fields, and swifts were screaming as they swooped in the sky. Ademar and his companions hoped to arrive before nightfall and as they urged the horses on, chalk dust puffed up under every hoof.

Ademar rode up to the castle with its strong outer walls, the blue and white striped Lusignan flags lying still in the heat of the day. His men were taking wary looks around them. Not so long ago this would not have been a visit on friendly, almost family terms. Ademar's steward bellowed up at the sentries on the walls, but they had already seen them and were opening the gates.

Ademar handed his horse to one of his men and strode towards the great hall. Hugh and Ralph were at the door, holding their arms wide in greeting. Hugh was all affability, clapping Ademar on the back. He tried not to scowl.

John had been up early and had strode about the grounds, taking in the Poitevin landscape, glorying in the right to be here as king. John, the runt of the litter, the spoilt baby of the family, born on Christmas Eve to Henry II and Eleanor of Aquitaine.

He punched one hand into the other in a sudden surge of rage as he remembered yet again the humiliation and his lack of prospects compared with his brothers. But his father's joke about Sansterre had turned around, and now John was king of the great empire, which stretched through England, across the Channel and reached south to Spain.

The visit to Lusignan was proving interesting, very interesting, and he was looking forward to talking to Ademar. He had plans for the Count of Angoulême and his family. Isabella would be married when the time was ripe – wasn't that what Hugh had hinted at? Or when the girl was ripe? Which would come first?

John's mind teemed with ideas, plots and suspicions; a stew of mistrust. The word had been given out that that he was riding to Portugal to seek a new bride, and a betrothal was possible now that he had been able to annul his marriage to his first wife. His thoughts skated over her. Avisa of Gloucester, another wealthy heiress – they had been married for ten years, no children. He would not let her marry again until he was good and ready. Her dowry of the earldom of Gloucester might be useful.

The young *infanta* in Portugal had looked like a suitable bride for a new English king. But Portugal was a long ride. Some of John's party had set off for the border, but he had turned back towards Angoulême and Poitiers.

Poitiers will always be important to me, Eleanor had written. *It was my birthplace, and my mother tongue was Poitevin.*

John smiled as he thought of his lively, intelligent and strong-willed mother, now in her late seventies and living in the abbey at Fontevraud, founded almost a hundred years ago. He had lived there too as a young boy. He had been sent there when his mother left England to return to rule Aquitaine.

He could dimly remember that time, when shouts and threats were hurled between his parents and had filled the palaces. Henry and Eleanor were both passionate, angry people, and Eleanor was furious with her husband's infidelities. The king's infatuations had lasted too long. Eleanor, full of scornful words, had been determined to fulfil her ambitions back in France, where she was a great duchess in her own right.

'I inherited Aquitaine when I was fifteen,' she reminded Henry, 'and was married to Louis VII, the son of the French king, by the time I was sixteen. That marriage did not break me, and nor will this one.'

'You were married to a monk, not a king, and were not that fond of the bookish boy in your bedchamber. I think you will find that his father wanted your territories, not you.'

She had divorced Louis, leaving their two daughters with him. Two months later Eleanor had married John's father, the young Henry, Count of Anjou and Duke of Normandy. He was nine years younger than her, energetic in battle and in bed.

Now she was a fierce old lady, left with one son – the youngest. She had thought it unlikely that John would become king, though it was true that their father had hoped that all of his four sons would help him rule such a widespread kingdom. He had made young Henry a joint King of England, ruling with him. Geoffrey had been made Duke of Brittany and Richard Duke of Aquitaine and Poitou, but there was nothing left for John. And now those three were all gone. Cold and gone, every one.

John growled to himself as he walked. 'Contrive and connive. Ademar must agree. We will pluck Isabella away from here. She is young and very desirable, and by the hooks of Christ, I want her. It can all come together – my kingdom, a marriage that will bring children, and we can make alliances together that once forged, will hold true.'

III

Lusignan, 1200

John returned to the great hall and slumped in a chair by the fireplace. The restless night and morning had not improved his temper. Now he was brooding, bitter. The fact was that without the Lusignans he would not have succeeded to the throne. True, his mother had helped and he had seen her diplomacy weaving its web again. She knew these independent Lusignan lords well; she spoke their *langue d'oc*, the Poitevin, and understood their hunger for land and power.

'Your succession is shaky, you need allies.' Her first words to him when he had arrived from Chinon. 'I think we can work on the Lusignans – an untrustworthy lot, but we could manage something, perhaps. Hugh was a great friend of Richard's – they fought together in the Crusades.'

John reflected sourly on his brother's friendships and the way he attracted people to his side.

'And he was always dangling La Marche before them, like a prize or a favour on the end of a sword. If they swore homage to you, bent their knee to you, we could give them La Marche.'

John knew that some said Hugh had kidnapped Eleanor on her ride south to Castile and held her until she agreed to give it to him. A story for the minstrels. But La Marche was an important piece of the patchwork. A Lusignan leaving for a crusade had sold all his lands and King Henry, ever astute, had bought La Marche. And then it had come to Richard, who made sure to keep it close. He needed this rich county for himself.

'Richard held onto it, even though he was friends with Hugh. He saw a need to save it lest it become a power base for vassals, and such turbulent vassals are bred in this part of the Poitevin! Such a hotchpotch of fiefdoms, such a mess of domains. Who really understands where any of their loyalties begin and end?'

King Philippe was deep in this balancing act too, promising La Marche to Ademar in return for his support against the English. But Philippe didn't own La Marche, or much territory at all. He depended on his vassal states and while these were a good buffer between his palace in Paris and the Angevin lands, his way south and west was blocked.

'Philippe will try to win over whomever he can, he will try to divide, he will try to find ways to end the English grip on this region. He is determined, so determined, and resolute, fierce and cunning, always looking for wavering loyalties. I recognise his tactics.'

So the truth was that Eleanor had persuaded John to give La Marche to Hugh – a slap in the face for the Count of Angoulême, but worth it. La Marche had served John's purposes well. In return for Hugh's support and homage John had granted him that rich, sprawling territory. The reward and gift from John to Hugh had tipped the balance of power in the succession dispute, and others had come over to John and deserted Arthur of Brittany.

His mother's advice was sound.

'The wrangling over that border territory of La Marche has rumbled back and forth between Hugh and Ademar for years. Now you must visit the Poitevin provinces, and for the sake of their peace and preservation, form an amicable league.'

Eleanor had said this as she lay on her bed in Fontevraud Abbey. She was fatigued, ageing at last in her seventy-seventh year. The journey she had made so recently had been tiring, riding back from Spain with her thirteen-year-old grand-daughter Blanche of Castile and witnessing her marriage to the twelve-year-old Louis, son of King Philippe of France. She had made sure of a diplomatic match there, choosing the bride herself.

Then she had to counsel John, the last of her sons, who had become his father's favourite in Henry's old age. And yet John had betrayed him, ganging up with Richard and the French king, hounding the old man from castle to castle until he died a broken man. John and Richard were constant con-spirators, so intent to the keep the crown within the family – the family that some called the Devil's Brood. Young Henry, Geoffrey of Brittany, Richard I of England and John.

'Arthur, damn his eyes.' John swore under his breath as he thought about Geoffrey's boy, his brother's boy – a pipsqueak of thirteen, a nuisance and disloyal. Geoffrey was dead before Arthur was born, and his mother Constance had remarried. It was rumoured she was with child, aged forty and not well. 'Arthur doesn't need a mother who encourages him to swear fealty to the French king – he needs a strong kinsman to show him what true family feeling is,' John snarled to himself. 'Even if we are a family that thrives on backstabbing, by all accounts.'

His harsh laugh echoed around the hall, his right hand tapping the arm of the chair. Bitter memories flooded back of conversations reported to him when William Marshall, his jus-ticar, so well-respected in England, had been woken with the news of Richard's death. Thank God for William Marshall! Able to quickly secure Rouen, the heart of Normandy, and able to take the news across the Seine to Archbishop Hubert Walter. This man was no friend, though. The Archbishop of

Canterbury had to be persuaded to sign up for John rather than Arthur.

'My lord Archbishop, we must make haste in choosing a king. The son is the nearest and closest in line of inheritance to a father and brother's lands.

'The nephew and grandson has a claim too, Prince Arthur is a rightful heir.'

'Arthur has treacherous advisors and is close to King Philippe. We must make this clear. And he is but a boy. A son has a better claim, an indubitable claim, and it is right that he should inherit.'

The archbishop reluctantly agreed.

'But you will never come to regret anything you do as much as what you're doing now.'

'Nonetheless, my advice is that it should be so.'

So William had cast his dice, and he'd swayed the barons in England and Normandy. Then John had set to work; flattered and wheedled those powerful barons who were against him: the barons of Brittany, Anjou and Maine. He had offered them positions of power, all part of an endless campaign to win them over. He'd made William des Roches Seneschal of Anjou. Des Roches had been the leader of the party who were all set on making a king out of Arthur, but he had switched sides with speed after that honour came his way. But the move angered John's old seneschal, Aimery de Thouars, and black with fury, he had switched to Arthur's camp.

Much good it did him. He backed the wrong horse, gloated John. But of course Aimery was related to Constance's new husband. John chewed at a thumbnail, worrying that there would be another set of family to subdue.

And there were still other problems. Arthur's sister Eleanor, the fair maid of Brittany, was fifteen, of marriageable age and yet still unmarried. She, like Arthur, had a strong claim to the English throne. Eleanor, her grandmother, had brought her up and hawked her half the way around Europe as an heiress worth having. Shame she was John's niece.

He laughed again and now thought with pleasure of Isabella, whom he had seen from his window that morning, walking in the herb garden. She was dressed simply in a thin grey gown of linen, embroidered with pansies, and twisting hyssop stalks together. Her hair was down, and as John watched he had a sudden longing to wrap it round her throat and take her there amongst the herb beds, to bend her backwards over one of those low stone walls. He stirred in his chair, lusty and angry.

John picked at a hangnail, working at it as he wrestled with thoughts about this marriage of Isabella and Hugh. Angoulême and Lusignan joined together – a huge cooperative fiefdom. This would be a powerful block, controlling the way south to Bordeaux and north to the Channel. They would have land that stretched across to the Atlantic coast at La Rochelle, a decent port with lucrative trade links. And with La Marche linking them on the eastern edges of this vast domain they could stop anyone travelling through France. It would be as easy as a pack of wolves taking a flock of sheep.

Yesterday evening as John had eaten and drunk into the night with the two brothers, Hugh and Ralph, it had all become much clearer how they saw their future – one of glory and riches, and all because of that twelve-year-old girl with her not-so-innocent eyes.

Hugh was keen to ensure that all was prepared and ready.

'Ademar will arrive tomorrow, and the Count of Limoges the next day. We can set up some flags and a dais for you to receive them. The oath of fealty must be observed by all.'

'I promise on my faith that I will in the future be faithful to the lord, never cause him harm, and will observe my homage to him completely, against all persons, in good faith and without deceit.' John recited the oath carelessly and threw out a hand to where a servant stood. More wine was poured.

'You will be pleased to see them here,' said Ralph cautiously. He had a new wife and new lands in Normandy. Richard had given him these and John had confirmed them. He was anxious to get back there without too much trouble.

'Yes, a fine pair they make! Two fractious nobles, full of rebellion. And brother Richard died at Châlus, one of Limoges' castles, shot by a crossbow. Trying to suppress that revolt against his authority cost him his life.'

'And Limoges' too – he died most unexpectedly. It is said that Richard's bastard saw to it.'

'And now the nephew is the new count, who rides to give you homage and be granted his rights by his overlord.'

'The first time either of them will have acknowledged an overlord,' put in Hugh. 'They found it difficult to swear to Richard.'

John smirked; it was indeed sweet to think of the implications for the counts of Angoulême and Limoges. Those two rebels bending a knee to him, the youngest son, Sansterre at birth because there wasn't a country left to give him. And now he had much land, many dukedoms, a kingdom to rule, to tax, to use and to plunder if he so desired. Thinking about lands again, fiefdoms and counties, brought him to his brooding mood, the one that had stayed with him all night and into the morning.

Voices cut through his dark thoughts, and Ademar was in front of him. John leant forward.

Ademar looked at the king to whom he must swear fealty. He was nothing like his brother. Richard had been six feet tall and full of majesty. John was neither of these. John was a typical Poitevin: short, dark red hair and a matching beard. Some might say he was barrel-chested, if they didn't want to be accused of flattery. And he had a bad-tempered air to him. Well, his father had been a king known for his fury and sudden huge rages – was this son like him? Ademar knelt and was almost immediately pulled to his feet by John, now smiling and restless.

Men marched into the hall carrying flags – first the royal standard with its three gold lions, shining on a red field: the lions of England, Normandy and Aquitaine. The Angoulême flag of red and gold diamonds came second, and the flags were held stout and still either side of John. Ademar knelt again, bareheaded and without his sword. His hands were clasped together as if in prayer, and he stretched them out towards John in submission. As a reluctant vassal he swore the oath of fealty.

John listened and watched, one eye drooping, his head propped on a clenched fist. He reached forward and took Ademar's hands. 'I accept your homage. Nothing is more important to a king than loyalty.'

When the brief ceremony closed there were murmurs from Hugh and Ralph. Approval? Satisfaction? Jubilation?

'Now let us find your daughter. She will be pleased to see you.'

John was halfway down the hall, full of anticipation; his face tense, his eyes fierce and dark. His mind was already running over Isabella, imagining her naked from nape to heels.

Isabella sat on a low wall in the herb garden, discarded herbs thrown onto the path. She was bored and anxious, waiting for her father to arrive. She picked at a loose thread in the embroidery on her dress. Pansies – they were for thoughts.

She knew there had been a ceremony, and that her father would now have John as his overlord. She also knew this would bring him some rights and duties – John would protect him if called upon, and Ademar must fight for John against his enemies. The Lusignans had been her father's enemies, but now she was to marry Hugh. He had been married before, but his wife had died.

She wished her mother were here. So stern and proud, but she always consoled Isabella with tales of their powerful relatives, kings of France, and the connections that linked so many families together and kept them strong. Isabella saw a small procession of men coming down the path: John with her father beside him, then Hugh and Ralph and a couple of servants at the back of the line. The herb paths were narrow and all of them were jostling together.

She stood up and met her father's eyes; he smiled at her and gestured towards John, who had pushed forward to be as close to Isabella as possible. His eyes were greedy and he put his hands around her waist and lifted her onto the wall calling out, 'Here is a herb full of grace, the fairest in this plot!' His hands slid around to her back, tickling her.

Her father laughed easily and Hugh, arriving next to him, agreed that Isabella was very fair, as beautiful as Helen, daughter of Zeus.

John lifted her down, making sure that his hands brushed against her as he placed her on the path in front of her father. Isabella, flushed and excited, bobbed a hasty curtsey and her father took her hand and drew her to him in a quick embrace. He whispered in her ear, 'Well done, you have made a conquest I think.'

Isabella looked at her feet and made a little gesture as if pushing something away. She wanted to talk to her father alone, but it seemed he was to be with John all morning discussing land boundaries.

'Agnes is waiting for you in the dairy.' Hugh's voice was an order to leave, so she smiled at them all and walked away. But her head was quickly bowed as she trailed down the path and her face unhappy.

The group of men broke up and John called to Ademar to come riding with him; they could talk as they rode. They were very close to his mother's favourite town, Poitiers, and he wanted to reassure her that all about was looking prosperous and safe.

'Hugh has done well to gain La Marche and your daughter. How soon will there be more children to boost the Lusignan numbers?'

'A while yet.' Ademar was reluctant to talk about Isabella and her future as a wife and mother. 'There is a son from his first marriage, and a daughter who is away in Pons, waiting to marry the count there. That will mark a good alliance, a stronghold on the way to the coast.'

John halted his horse and turned to Ademar. 'Ah yes, alliances, alliances – that is what is all about, but I am more and more against this one. La Marche added to Lusignan, added to Angoulême, and now you tell me there is a Lusignan daughter marrying into the far west border! How do I begin to trust that this region will be true to the Angevins, to me, and not go twisting and turning towards Paris? And then there is Isabella.'

John broke off and wheeled his horse around. His loss of temper had unsettled it, and now in a fury he pulled hard on the reins. Ademar waited and then John began again.

'Ademar, Hugh le Brun, this Lord of Lusignan, is not going to marry Isabella – this dangerous development will not be allowed to happen. *I* am going to marry Isabella, and you are going to help me get her away from here.'

Ademar's amazed stare made John roar, a mixture of laughter and anger.

'You don't believe me? Think about it – your daughter, Queen of England, not Countess of La Marche. Oh, I know she will inherit Angoulême too, but the English crown is a far better prospect, a far better alliance.'

Was this true? Did he mean this? What in God's truth

would happen now? Ademar could see how well this would sit, how pleased Alice would be. And it would be a huge blow to the Lusignans, with their territory diminished, humiliation heaped on their heads. Brave, powerful Hugh – what a blow to his dignity.

'I will send Hugh to England to find out about some matters pertaining to my mother's widow dowry,' John continued. 'You can tell Isabella a story, and you can tell it to Ralph after Hugh has left. Tell Isabella that I will come to Angoulême, I grant you, not as planned, but to take in a day of high ceremony in which you and the whole of your family must pay homage for Angoulême to me as Duke of Aquitaine.'

Yes, thought Ademar, John was Duke of Aquitaine and had been crowned King of England in London. He had taken hold of this great kingdom and was no more the poverty-stricken Lackland. Ademar knew that John's first move after Richard's death had been to ride to Chinon and secure the treasury. He thought quickly ahead to the next few days.

'I will tell Hugh that you have commanded this ceremony, that I was counselled by Alice to obey any demand from you if all went well here,' he said eventually. 'I will ride home and take Isabella with me.'

John nodded. 'When I have made the tour of places I have to control, and make sure I will follow. There are messages to be sent to my party in Portugal – there will be no bride to bring home from Sancho's court. I find Isabella very captivating, very captivating indeed.'

'She is still very young. Her mother thinks she is not ready for the marriage bed.'

But John was already cantering away, back to the castle.

IV

Blue flags with three gold lions had been added to the great hall. Men in blue and gold tabards had ridden in through the gates and swarmed about the yard. The Viscount of Limoges had arrived, Ademar's kinsman and the nephew of the man whose castle had been besieged by Richard. He was another local Poitevin lord who did not like authority. He swaggered up to the dais and went through the oath ceremony as John restored his rights and property. Like the Lusignans and Ademar, his feudal obligations did not run particularly deep or true.

Disorder and rebellion were engrained in these men, John thought. After all, Richard had met his death fighting the rebels of Aquitaine at Châlus, besieging that castle in the Limousin fiefdom. His guts and brain were buried there, his heart in Rouen and the rest of him at the feet of his father Henry's tomb in Fontevraud. Richard had died in Eleanor's arms. Something more for John to brood about.

'I hear it was a story of treasure that took Richard to Châlus.' John was casual and unconcerned, but he wanted to hear from Limoges, and what was being said. It had all happened just over a year ago, that festering wound that pulled down the Lionheart.

'A ploughman turned over a pot, full of gold coins from the

46

time before Charlemagne – they had Caesar's head on them,' Limoges explained. 'Everyone thought these coins were worth more than they were, including Richard who arrived accusing my uncle of cheating him of the treasure. The castle at Châlus was in poor repair, easy to attack or besiege.'

'And?'

'Richard was walking about, taking sights on its defences, noting the weakness of the walls – the castle could be breached with ease. But there was a crossbowman watching him from the ramparts and he took a shot at Richard. The bolt caught him in the shoulder. He wore no armour, we discovered later – he was so sure of himself.' Limoges shook his head and slapped at the fruit flies which clustered around the dish of grapes they were sharing.

'I hear his captain, the mercenary Mercadier, dealt with the crossbowman. Flayed him alive, is that what was done?'

'Indeed it was. We know Mercadier – he fought against Limoges before. Fifteen years ago he attacked the city and turned the country to wasteland. A man of great cruelty, and able to strike terror wherever he rides.'

'Dead now.' John leant back and looked long and hard at Limoges. 'He was killed in Bordeaux on Easter Monday. He wanted to pay homage to my mother on her way back from Spain. A rival assassinated him.'

A pause as Limoges wondered desperately if he was being implicated in this murder, but John was already bored with the story. Nothing new had been spoken of; there were no twists in this tale of his brother's death. He needed to talk to Ademar. Several days had passed since their ride together and it was time to put the plan to work.

The feasting and hunting had created a nice lull, a small holiday for the soldiers and groomsmen, but John was becoming restless. He had thrown himself into the hunts and feasts that followed the ceremonies; a welcome distraction and

47

a good cover for the need to be here to work out the details of his plans for Isabella and Angoulême. But now he must try to mix policy and passion – a difficult brew to control.

Containing himself did not suit at all. He had grabbed the wrist of a dairymaid the evening before, as she scurried back from the great hall, twisting it hard until she winced and exclaimed with the pain. His eyes slid over her. Young, a bit flushed, nervous eyes. She would do. Isabella was not to be touched yet. This girl he fondled roughly, pushing her back against the wall and pulling up her skirt. It had all been over very quickly and he left her snivelling into her coarse apron.

Isabella, on her way to her chamber, stood with one hand over her mouth, the other holding it there to stop the scream escaping, and watched from the shadowy corner of the keep wall. She tried not to breathe, to see, to hear. But she did all of those, and some part of her, some distant, uncontrollable part of her, was excited and disturbed. She had crept up to her room, still with one hand over her mouth.

'Isabella!' Agnes rushed to her side. 'You feel very cold. Are you sickening with a fever?' She did not wait for a reply, but hurried Isabella into her bed. Isabella lay there, pale and quiet. Agnes brought her an infusion of herbs and persuaded her to drink. Then she slipped into her own pallet bed, turned over once or twice and was asleep. Isabella stared into the dark, hugging herself, until she too slept.

The kitchen men groaned under the burden of the preparation of food for so many; and not only food, but water to heat for washing. Everyone was taking advantage of the hot, dry summer days to strip off and wash. Some of the men dragged a wooden tub into the yard and washed there.

'You can wash in the well water without the benefit of heat,' the bathman grumbled at them. 'Be glad the days are so warm.' He had heated cauldrons of water to add to the wooden tubs of cold well water for those washing in their rooms in the castle. Like the soldiers, everyone was intent on a bath – there might not be another chance for some weeks.

'Is it true there is a bathhouse in Angoulême?' asked one of the young Lusignan kitchen boys. 'I have heard they are places that begin to make you dimpled, soft and weak.'

'They are places that can make parts of you very hard and strong,' called a man. 'Full of lewd women who will feed you as you bathe, or give you wine and sponge you down for a price.'

'The bathhouse in Limoges has six beds to fall into after you are dry,' added another man. 'Hangings of curtains all round to keep out the chill and keep in the blessed warmth. A good place to visit in the winter months. My lady gives those she favours gifts of a hot bath.'

Agnes walked across the yard, her face averted. She did not want to enter into conversation with these men who had filled Lusignan with noise and clamour from dawn to dusk. She had been to the herb garden to pick parsley and chives for the dairy, where Isabella was supposed to be learning about butter and the use of curds in sweet desserts. All the women were helping to make extra cheese, using goats' milk and wrapping the crottins in chestnut leaves or rolling them in wood ash.

Isabella had made curds, and put them in a muslin bag on a rush mat to drain. She dared not look at Bess, the dairymaid her own age, who was sitting dull in the corner as if she was not of this world. She wanted to ask her questions, yet dared not. She wanted to hiss at her and scratch her face. She wanted to take her hand and run her through the castle grounds shouting, 'Look at her who John took and spoilt – it ill becomes the king to behave so.'

She turned to Agnes, pushing at her crossly. 'I feel unwell,

I must go to my room now.' And she left the low, cool dairy and crossed into the heat of the courtyard, then up the spiral steps to her chamber where she lay on her bed and wept.

The next day Lusignan was in confusion bordering on disorder. John was up early and wasted no time giving orders. His men, who had been idly standing around in the stable yard, enjoying the sun and flirting with the dairymaids, found themselves being yelled at and harangued.

'We are leaving for Cognac tomorrow – get everything ready and make sure you leave nothing behind. Pack up my baggage train.'

Hugh le Brun was gripped by the arm and led to the ramparts, where John gestured towards the north.

'I want you to do something for me. I want you to ride north and visit William Marshall in London. My mother's dowry, her widow's dowry, has not been sent in recent months. William will know what to do but I need someone to help sort out the mess.'

Hugh gazed across the fields and thought hard. This was a singular honour, being chosen to arbitrate on John's behalf, and Eleanor's too. It would be useful to be seen to be trusted. 'I will do so, my lord. Will you write to William Marshall?'

'Yes, yes – at once, and you must leave as soon as I have written.'

And with that, he was already striding back to the castle door, calling for parchment and a scribe to help him write to Marshall.

Later, as Hugh readied his baggage for the journey, the letter was brought to him. He glanced at it: hastily written, hastily read, but important for his journey to London.

We command you to allow Hugh le Brun, the IX of Lusignan, to speak with William Marshall, Justicar of England, and

*by this countersign so you may credit him in this business.
Witnessed by myself at Lusignan, 15 July in the second year
of our reign.*

Hugh was helping to saddle the horses and giving instructions to Ralph at the same time. 'This is a serious mission I am being sent on. He says his mother's dowry has been compromised, but that William Marshall will help to make it right. It needs a visit from a good friend to help. Make sure John leaves here in a pleasant mood.'

Ralph looked worried. 'I only have today before he leaves. He has been hunting, and we have no other entertainment for him.'

'Minstrels? We have some minstrels, Ralph, they can sing tonight and then tomorrow he leaves with the sound of singing in his memory. It would be calming.'

Ralph watched his brother ride away, two servants accompanying him, and turned to the hall to find the minstrels sprawled in a corner, playing cards.

'Tonight we will have juggling and then something brave, not a rude, rustic song.'

'We could sing *The Song of Roland* that was sung to frighten the English a hundred years ago.'

'John will not be frightened – he's not English enough! But the song is a good choice: loyalty and fealty figure large in those verses.'

The trio scrambled to their feet and began rehearsing. They knew the *chanson de geste* off by heart but they often improvised, changing lines about, adding a new chorus here and there. It was good to be using the Occitan language to create the stories of earlier times – the heroes and villains would live and die again tonight.

Next Ralph ordered the evening banquet, the great supper to be eaten by all. It was gluttony to be frowned on,

51

no doubt, but with a king and neighbouring counts to feed, and all their men and all the servants, it had better be done. And would Ademar want Isabella to sit with him before he returned to Angoulême? It was not usual for her to attend the evening banquets, Ralph fretted as he planned the day. It would have to be simpler this time; the kitchen and cooks were very busy with all these extra people.

He sighed as he left the kitchen. He was uneasy having John, Limoges and Ademar in Lusignan. He would be glad when they left and he could begin to plan his journey back to Normandy and to his young, heavily pregnant wife.

Agnes combed Isabella's hair and wound it around her head, then let it drop onto her shoulders.

'You look pale, but no fever. Another feast tonight – Father Benedict will not be pleased that all are eating such rich meals.'

Isabella was not listening. She wondered if she could find her father now and talk to him alone. He had come back from riding again with John, she knew that, and Hugh had left for England. He had bid her farewell in a very fond but distracted manner, and she knew that he was pleased to have been given this task by John. He had told her to listen to Agnes and Ralph, and that she should write to her mother so that Ademar could take the letter back with him. The scribe would help her. And then, he added, it may be possible for their marriage to take place on his return, and he held her close for a moment after he said this.

'Tomorrow? We are to leave tomorrow?' Isabella looked at her father in amazement, 'But I am to stay here until I marry Hugh. That is what you told me, and mother has written that she is looking to the wedding day when she will see me again.'

Ademar had come into her room, closing the door very firmly before he told Isabella the news. 'John has ordered us both to return to Angoulême, where the entire family of the counts of

Angoulême, the Taillefer family – that is, myself, your mother the Countess Alice and you – will swear an oath of fealty.'

Isabella turned away. This was bewildering, unsettling news. John had ordered her to return with her father? But what was this oath about? Had not her father sworn one here, only a few days ago? And her mother would not be pleased to have to humble herself.

Agnes stood quietly. To go back to Angoulême would be a rare pleasure: she had not expected to be able to see her family again for several months. She knew John was riding to Cognac tomorrow, she had heard that in the kitchen when she went fetch hot water.

'You will have to pack the clothes chests, Agnes, and take the small one too. Isabella will need her precious things.' Ademar walked to the window and looked out at Lusignan: a rich, important fiefdom indeed, but the English crown was far richer, far more important. He rubbed his hands together and looked forward to telling Alice and Isabella of the new fortune that would come their way. 'It will be a long ride tomorrow. We will start at dawn, but even so we will have to break the journey. I must talk to the grooms.'

Then Ademar was gone, leaving Isabella and Agnes to begin packing. Agnes folded linen, cloaks, veils and caps into the larger of the two chests. Isabella sat on the bed and watched her.

'Come on, look through the chest and make sure you have everything you need,' Agnes urged her. 'I expect we will be back here again in a few weeks but you will need to take most of your clothes.'

John liked the idea of the whole Angoulême family together in their domain, making the oath with empty, outstretched hands. But this thought was only part of a plot – this was what Isabella was being told, it was what Ademar would tell Ralph when John had left. Tonight there would be a feast, some minstrel entertainment, and then tomorrow he would leave. He would travel to Cognac, and he would need to visit other places too – Bordeaux, Gascony, Périgueux – making sure that the loyalty to him was holding in this large, sprawling, independent region.

He walked with Ralph along the parapets, following the walls that skirted the courtyard.

Ralph listened to John's impatient voice as he explained his journey so far; the chasing about the countryside after signing the treaty with King Philippe to ensure that he, John, was recognised as heir to his brother. Normandy was the sticking point. It was in Normandy at the beginning of the year that the Lusignan brothers had sworn fealty. The most important family from the southwest on his side, and some said the most treacherous.

'We are the Angevin kings of England – we are Norman dukes as well, and have much claim to French lands. But Philippe wants to be the overlord of Normandy and since that treaty he is, but he supports me, not Arthur, he recognises me, not Arthur.' John was triumphant. 'Once and for all, it is settled. I am the King of England, Duke of Anjou, Duke of Brittany and will be the Duke of Aquitaine when...'

His voice trailed off. When his mother died was his thought, Ralph's too, but when his mother died the region could become less loyal to a son, and they both knew this.

'And Brittany?' asked Ralph. He knew Brittany was important: Arthur was from there and wanted to rule it, as his father had done.

'Brittany – well, I had to pay for Brittany, a sum that the treasury saw as extortionate and so did I, but it keeps it in the family!' Again John's harsh, barking laugh. 'It is yet to be paid, and the release of so much silver might be difficult for all concerned.'

*

The great hall was ready for a feast again, trestle tables set with white cloths and benches pushed in under them. A massive chair for John had been placed at the end of one of the tables – usually Hugh sat here. The floor had been swept and new rushes strewn, but these could not disguise the mess of grease and bone fragments that stubbornly coated the stone. Tallow candles would be lit if the feast went on into the night, but now they were into the summer the light lasted until later.

People thronged in and began to sit. John was slouched in the chair, Ralph on one side, Ademar on the other. Limoges sat by Ralph, fiddling with his belt buckle – the rich meals were beginning to thicken his waist. There was no sign of Isabella.

Servants brought the dishes in, placing them down the trestles. Several rabbits, quartered and cooked in red wine, some new carrots and onions dressed in butter and chives, pieces of veal with cloves and prunes, coloured and fragrant with saffron and sprinkled with almonds. There was a potage of broad beans, young turnips and bacon, thickened with bread to fill up any spaces. Freshwater crayfish from the river had been boiled and set in mounds. Bread was piled high all along the tables. For something sweet there were circles of pastry, fried and smothered in honey, with huge bowls of cherries to add at will.

'Is Isabella not joining us?'

Ademar shook his head. 'She needs to rest,' he explained very quietly, so that Ralph could not hear. 'It will be a long ride tomorrow.'

'A pity – she would have enjoyed the cherries, I think. They are good this season. Ripe cherries need to be gathered.'

John's meaning was very clear to Ademar, who thought again of the prestige, the honour and the pride in having a daughter as Queen of England.

The minstrels arrived, capering and juggling with fruit and wooden balls. They began their *Song of Roland* near John, the verses and their haunting chorus stilling the gathering. The treachery and vindictive character of Ganelon, the might of Charlemagne and the enormous courage of Roland, blowing his oliphant horn to summon help as he beat off the Saracen hordes, lived once more. It was full of action, a great epic.

Lines lingered in the minds of the men who listened: *conquered the land and won the western main, now no fortress against him doth remain.*

In the morning, John left before first light, the men and horses impatient to be away for there were many miles to travel in the next few weeks. Limoges left soon after him, his blue and gold livery echoing the sky and the corn.

Ademar found Ralph in the stable yard, checking the stores. After so many mouths had been fed there was a need to replenish oats and barley. Thank Heaven it was an abundant harvest this year, the best anyone could wish for. The hay would be stacked high for the winter feed.

'Ralph, I am returning to Angoulême now and I wish to take Isabella back there for a few days. John will call on us as he rides north after he visits Périgueux. Indeed, he wishes to visit our stronghold, and to see Alice bend her knee – Isabella too. She can ride with me as an escort. You have no objection to Isabella returning to her home? We can arrange the journey back here when Hugh returns from England.'

'It is irregular,' said Ralph stiffly. 'I would rather she stayed here under my care while Hugh is gone. Is it really necessary for her to swear fealty to John in Angoulême?'

'John is intent on binding the whole family to him. If we swear allegiance together, all very public and in the town itself, he thinks this will make it difficult to break. He seems determined to make us recognise that we are his vassals now.

Alice will not like it but she will do it. And of course, with Isabella being the heiress she has to show submission too.'

This was a strong argument, but Ralph was still unsure. 'But returning with you seems a hasty move.' Ralph paced about the yard, thinking. 'I would wish Isabella to stay here in Lusignan. Once betrothed it is not good to return home, unless it is for the wedding day.'

'She has exchanged the *verba de praesenti*, those binding vows, with Hugh. And besides, her mother wishes to see her and talk to her about women's matters. She needs to see her. There are plans to be made.' This last sentence was full of meaning. Plans for a wedding day, both men thought, but Ademar was not thinking of Hugh and Isabella. He tried hard to conceal his gloating pride as he spoke.

Yes, Ralph thought, John would do well to bind you to him again – you have been treacherous in the past. And yes, Isabella is nearing the time when she can be married and take her place with Hugh in all things. Hugh will want to marry her in church; it would be indecent otherwise. Her mother will want to talk about that. He stopped frowning and began to think with more cheer about a future with Isabella, Countess of Lusignan.

The small party rode out of the gate and across to the road and tracks that would take them south to Angoulême, about a two-day ride, with Isabella on a Spanish *jennet*. Small and quiet, this horse was better for the long journey than a pony, and it had been good of Ralph to offer it to her.

A cart held the baggage and bundles and Agnes perched among them, wrapping her cloak around her in the pale dawn light. She steadied herself, putting out a hand to the small chest. She remembered it being made, the oak and cedar planks being cut and edged before the carpenter pegged them together and then strapped the chest in iron and leather.

Agnes had lifted the flat, heavy lid and dropped in bunches of lavender to keep away the moths. The chest was intended for small treasures: letters, folded silks – Isabella's circlet of gold filigree was wrapped in one of these.

Agnes bit her lip as she watched the group assemble. There was something in the air, something stirring under the surface of this journey that made her anxious.

Young Hugh had helped to saddle the small horse and led Isabella around the yard as she readied herself. She was keyed up, he thought; she looked as if she was about to go hunting, not for an arduous ride home.

'He is a good mount, his gait is smooth and you should manage well.'

'We can hunt with him when I return?'

'I will look to that – we will have the dogs trained by then.'

And then they were gone. Hugh, working in the stables, grooming his pony, thought: Lusignan is quiet now. No Father, no Limoges, no Ademar, no John, no Isabella.

V

Angoulême, July and August 1200

Agnes sat with her parents in the solar, beaming at their surprise. Her father stood, tall and beefy, listening to her excited stories of Lusignan and King John. Her mother, Emma Roussie, stooped and mouselike, sat by her, patting her hand. She was pleased to see Agnes again: a daughter who had done well, a companion to Isabella and respected by the Taillefer family as industrious and loyal.

The solar hall and the chambers, with their stone walls and recessed windows, were above the ground floor, which was a warehouse for the cloth that her father traded. Bernard Roussie was a shrewd businessman and with the help of his wife's family had built a prosperous trading enterprise. He appreciated all that the Count of Angoulême did to keep the town safe, and that he had secured the routes to the coast: La Rochelle, Bordeaux, Royan – important ports for the merchants.

'And King John will come to Angoulême – he shouted at all the servants that they had to be ready for a tour of all the towns south of here, but that he would make his way back to Angoulême,' Agnes declared. 'It was an unexpected way to return.'

'I thought he had it in mind to marry a daughter of the

King of the Portuguese,' Bernard replied. 'A party of John's came riding near La Rochelle on their way to the border last month when I took delivery of silk from Italy. He had some great nobles readied to bring him back a bride. Does he mean to bring her here?'

'There was no mention of the Portuguese. I think he is looking closer to home now.' Agnes glanced at her father, and hesitated before continuing. 'The plain truth is that he was full of heat whenever he saw Isabella. Oh, he tried to pretend it was just a game, the way he was with her, but it was serious. And he was so full of passion he could not contain his blood and meddled with a dairymaid. I have reason to believe that Isabella saw something of that: she was sick that night and in the morning, sick with fear.'

Bernard put out a hand to help his wife to her feet; she had turned frightened eyes to him as Agnes spoke.

'Should we tell someone of this plan of John's? Will the Lusignans know what is seething in their midst? And Ademar and Alice how will they behave if John wants Isabella? She has been promised – more than promised – to Hugh, it is to make our lands strong and safe.' Emma's anxious voice trailed away as both her daughter and her husband held her arms and helped her to her bed. She looked up at them, so full of purpose and so dear to her. All she wanted was to be quiet and peaceful, not disturbed by news of trouble and discord.

Bernard did not speak again until he was sure that Emma could not hear him.

'It will be something that the Count of Angoulême will know, of that I am sure. Did he speak of this to anyone on the ride home?'

Agnes shook her head, but she remembered how pleased Ademar had been with the news of John's visit to Angoulême, more pleased than if the visit was only a plan to make sure that the Count of Angoulême and his family paid homage. Perhaps Ademar did know? He must have noticed the king's face when he looked at Isabella, been proud and pleased that his daughter was noticed and admired.

Bernard left the room, and Agnes sat on a stool by her mother's side and told her to sleep and not to worry: she would organise the kitchens and help with the stock-keeping while she could. She would set things in order before she had to leave for the castle and Isabella's care. To have been given two days to spend with her parents was a reward for her faithful service, but she had to return to the Taillefers. Her life was at Isabella's side.

Ademar grasped Alice's hands and turned her to the window to look out, as they did on so many mornings.

'What do you see, wife? Do you see the three counties linked together and Isabella and Hugh with their triumphant marriage, a solid domain made sure and our place in the Poitevin kissed by the sun?'

Alice shook herself free and turned back to see Ademar's face. He looked so full of pride, he looked like the master whose ram or bull has made good money at the spring fair. 'You are telling me about our daughter and Hugh and the outcome of their union, but something else is in your eyes.'

'I have news of a union that will make Isabella the Queen of England, will make a grandson a King of England, and will make us the family whose place is more than Poitevin, more than Paris. John will marry Isabella: he will arrive here and marry her here.'

Alice said nothing, holding in the cry of surprise, the delight and the victory.

Ademar nodded at her; he was exultant now he had told her. 'He was captured by her beauty and spirit when he saw her that first evening. When we rode together it was a device so that he could tell me – he was so eager to tell me that he had planned a way to send Hugh out of France, and that I must arrange for Isabella to travel back here with me. It was not that hard to persuade Ralph – he fussed about it but I reminded him of the betrothal and the binding vows and reassured him that all would be well. His consent was easily given: Ralph is no barrier to a strong voice.'

'But Hugh might be. He will find this most ill-becoming, a humiliation and a betrayal. When is he expected to return?'

'When the task in London is carried out and when the winds are favourable for the Channel. We are not sure but it will be some weeks yet.'

'And John arrives here?'

'After his visit to Gascony, then Périgueux, then here. Sometime towards the end of August.'

'And Isabella? You have given her no hint of this? No sly sentence?'

'No, we will tell her together and prepare her for her life ahead. Agnes will be back here soon and she can help. I think Isabella found Hugh very comfortable, and Lusignan was becoming a friendly place for her. What lies ahead will be different and...'

'Difficult,' added Alice. 'John has a reputation like his father before him, we well know that – bastard children and a hot temper. He can be full of anger and ill will.'

'But the triumph of our daughter being married to the King of England! The glory and the honour, Alice, it is more than we could hope for.'

'She is still young. Hugh waited – John will not wait.'

Ademar frowned and then laughed. 'Well, she will not be the first to go to a marriage bed at such an age. She is old enough to consent to the marriage, and we can be sure that she will. There will be no need to coerce our daughter into this union.'

They found Isabella in her chamber, chattering to a group of young women; girls like her, some of them giggling as Isabella told them one of the stories she had been told in Lusignan. She jumped up, flushed with excitement. Her mother dismissed the group with a stern face and they sped out of the door and down the spiral stone steps.

'Isabella, your father has news for you. Important news.'

Everything was shown in Ademar's face; he was so full of pride and confidence that he seemed to have grown in stature. Isabella stepped forward, her eyes fixed on him.

'King John is to marry you, Isabella. He will ride here after Périgueux and we will have a ceremony in the cathedral before he takes you as his bride to Chinon, where more will take place. I believe he is to bring the Archbishop of Bordeaux with him for the purpose.'

Isabella sank to her knees, a silent cry covered with both hands.

'Stand up! You will be Queen of England, a woman who will be the mother of kings, important and powerful.'

Isabella stood and Alice swooped on her, holding her by the elbow and hissing, 'Understand this: he has made it known that he wants you for his wife, and that is how it will be. You will marry him as soon as he arrives with the archbishop and accompany him to England for a coronation. A coronation! Isabella, you will be crowned the Queen of England.'

'But I am betrothed to Hugh! I am to live in Lusignan and our lands will be joined together and our families will be allied! Mother, I am to live near Angoulême, a few days' ride away, and be close to my home. One day Angoulême will belong to me and—'

'It will still be yours whomever you marry, but so much more will be yours too. There are bound to be great dowry lands given to you as the king's wife.'

Isabella wept, she felt torn apart by such conflict. She had seen John's behaviour when he wanted something, felt the cruelty and anger that slid about under his surface, knew that this man was not kind, not a knight of chivalry as Hugh was. Oh, the Lusignans were treacherous, and so were the counts of Angoulême – this she understood but she knew that John was casually callous, and that for him she could be – would be – a plaything.

'Have you no ambition? This is a marriage that will bring great triumph to our family.' Her father signalled to Alice that he was leaving her to deal with the problem of Isabella's reluctance. 'Find a way to make her see sense. She has little choice but I do not want a crumpled heap delivered to John. He fell for her spirit, not this wailing.'

After Ademar had left the room Alice walked Isabella around the room, cajoling, explaining and commanding. Her arguments were forceful and fierce; she had not expected this resistance from Isabella.

'And you will have gowns and jewels that are only given to queens. Do not think of being apart from us, this is not how our family thinks. We are brave and powerful and strong. I have royal blood and so do you, Isabella, and now you will bring royal sons into the world. It is an unheard of glory for the Taillefers – our long line of greatness stretches back and will now advance into the future. It is the summit of your father's ambition that this has come about, and it should be yours too. So young and so full of glory, but I fear you are still naïve.'

Perhaps she should console her daughter? Perhaps she needed to know that there would be some friends with her? In Lusignan Agnes had accompanied Isabella; she would need to have Agnes about her again.

'Agnes will come with you – you will need a maid and companion from your own land when you leave here, and at your age you need someone to help you who knows you well.'

'The king makes mischief for people my age,' whispered Isabella bitterly. But she knew her mother was not listening.

Alice hurried on to the other consoling idea about being queen. 'Think of your position at court: there will be much honour and much respect given to you, far more than as Countess of Lusignan or La Marche! Think of your title! Being a queen is forever.'

Alice sat Isabella on the stool by her bed. 'You know that the marriage bed will be a place of union between John and you. His first wife had no children. All to the good if you have them early on.'

'Mother, I fear I will not.' Isabella dared not look up.

'Then they will come to you later, but come they will – John is more than capable of fathering and you are of good stock. I see many children in your future.'

Isabella stared at the wall and shuddered. But to have a son who was a king was certainly something to celebrate, and if she as queen were a mother of sons, what authority she would have! She thought of Lusignan and the well-ordered life there, a life she understood well even if the training to be mistress of it all was tedious. Hugh had promised her so much for when she grew older, and he seemed to expect that she would grow wiser too. Then she thought of John and the way he had looked at her and touched her, her very soul aroused, her very being tempted. And what she had seen in the courtyard when he had taken Bess against the wall – terrifying and dreadful. She shook her head at the memory. How would she ever forget? It had sickened her, but there was fascination too. That was what appalled her: the arousal that it had brought about. She shook her head again. No one knew, she could tell no one – her mother would be dismissive. Her mother had already moved on to planning what Isabella would wear when John arrived.

'We will ask Bernard Roussie if he has new silks we can

sew into gowns for you. For your wedding day we will need something of deepest blue, but when John first sees you again, I think a rich, dark, wine red would be appropriate and appreciated. I will order Agnes to come back to the castle and bring silks with her.'

Bernard and Agnes walked through the narrow alleys that wound around the town, only one stride across. A few houses had windows, just small, thin, dirty panes of glass or greasy linen. Two servants walked behind, carrying the bales of cloth. Agnes was pleased to be summoned back; she needed to see Isabella and to find out the truth behind the king's visit. She was sure her observations were true, but what was to be the outcome? Her father had decided that whatever happened it would be good for Angoulême and, he hoped, for the surrounding countryside. He was not one for subterfuge and gossip.

Isabella exclaimed over the silks and damask, the linen and the fur. Alice examined them carefully and chose the deep red that she had promised would show Isabella at her most mature, and then she picked out the gold brocade that would be used in the sleeves and overskirt. Agnes helped her father pack the cloth away and he, Alice and the Roussie servants disappeared to haggle over lengths and prices.

Isabella looked at Agnes, her face tight with news.

'Shall we walk about and tell each other secrets?'

'I have no secrets anymore, my stories from Lusignan have all been told to the maids. They were amazed to hear of Melusine, but not as amazed as I had been. I do not tell the story as well as old Joan. And now I will never give birth to a Lusignan, and Melusine will not fly over the castle to tell the world of a new child.'

So it was true: Isabella was to marry John, and Hugh was to be betrayed.

'John is to come here soon and we will be married, and then I will ride with him to Chinon for more ceremony and the marriage bed, and after that we will cross to England. There is to be a coronation in Westminster – my father and mother are so full of pride they can hardly speak when they look at me. They do not see me at all!'

Agnes took her hand and held it tight. 'Are you frightened? Did John meddle with you in Lusignan?'

'No. He touched me, told me that I was beautiful and stroked me, but he spoke softly, he treated me with soft touches, he was not brutal as…' Isabella broke off and then continued. 'But he knows that he will have me for his bride, for his wife and as the mother of his children. He wants this to be, and so it will.'

'And you, Isabella – you have always been telling me how many titles you will have, how grand you will be. How grand you will be as queen! This pleases you?'

Isabella looked down and then up. She turned away from Agnes and then back again. 'Agnes, I marvel at what is about to happen. The will of the king is forceful. I cannot rage and oppose my parents or him. But I will be queen! Think of that: Queen of England.' Isabella whirled around the room, her skirt flying, and when she returned to where Agnes stood she seized her hand. 'And you, Agnes, you will come with me and be my lady at court for the new queen. The court will be a place where I can do what I please as queen: I will have lands and a dowry, great honour.'

Agnes observed the flushed cheeks and bright eyes, the note of desperate gaiety in Isabella. Yes, she would be queen, and she would enjoy all the magnificence that it brought. Her vanity had been engaged, and spoilt as she was by her life in both Angoulême and Lusignan, Isabella responded to the flattery and the promises. Well, if Agnes was to go with her to England some new dresses would be hers, too: her father would be pleased to see her wearing the best he could provide. But this seemed a poor exchange for leaving her family so far behind.

Together they unpacked the two chests brought with them from Lusignan. Agnes lifted out the gold guirland and placed it on Isabella's head.

'You must practise wearing a crown,' she said, and curtsied.

The days passed in preparation. Isabella was made three new gowns; Agnes suggested a thick woollen cloak too, for it was well known that England was cold and damp. Her father had traded north and he had some small pelts of grey-white fur from the kingdom of Hungary; it was decided to use these as a trim for the hood.

'Not for you, Agnes, too rich for you, but I will make sure your cloak is the best cloth I can find.'

Agnes stroked the fur and smiled.

A messenger arrived. John was in Périgueux, a day's ride away, and he would be in Angoulême the following day: the 23rd of August.

There was uproar – rooms were swept, windows wiped and fresh rushes cut for the floor of the dining hall. The kitchen men sweated as they cut up boar and deer, ready to roast. The ripe orchard fruit was picked and prepared for compotes and pies. Alice, imperious and demanding, was everywhere and Isabella walked with her, noting the way her mother rasped her orders and made people scurry before her. This was how to control and use power. She nodded to herself; she would be like her mother, and in future show far greater authority. Her steps became a mimic of determination and she relished the thought. This marriage to John would become a triumph. She would not make an enemy of him, frightened though she was.

VI

Angoulême, August 1200

John's party rode through the forests towards Angoulême, with the expectation of a good welcome in that rich hilltop town. The nobles who had been on the mission to Portugal had joined him, turned back at the border in time to avoid a heavy diplomatic error. John was pleased to see Peter des Roches.

'How lightly these vassals have chosen to wear their feudal obligations. So turbulent, so money-minded, always looking for trouble, and the further south you go, so cynical and so full of bragging. Well, my army has shown them I have power – they must respect that. And the fiefdoms were worth visiting: disorder is a constant threat.'

'Treacherous and rebellious though they are, it seems you have forced them to give you a peaceable welcome. Let us hope it is of lasting value. And what of the Lusignans? Will you deal with them when they find that you have snatched Isabella from them?'

John laughed. 'Maybe I will be generous towards them with land treaties in exchange for their betrothed. That would be something that Hugh would appreciate. They say no good ever came from a king who lives north of the Loire. We'll see if we can make them change their minds.'

They clattered up to the castle, careless with their greetings. John was eager to see Ademar; Isabella must be ready for this hasty wedding.

She stood next to her father, her shoulders bare, long sleeves sweeping her sides, her gathered skirt of red and gold, the colours of Angoulême, skimming her body. She was wrapped in sumptuous silk and brocade: a gift and a bride for a king. John bent over her and whispered in her ear, and her mother saw the blush and the smile. Had he promised her the crown and honour, or were they words of love?

Armed men moved around the hall, Peter des Roches taking in the place that he knew well. He had been given great authority before by Richard, as a clerk and member of the king's chamber, and now John had made him treasurer of St Hilaire le Grand, an important church in Poitiers. Ademar watched him sourly. He might be helping himself to favours hereabouts, but he was no Poitevin. Des Roches was from Tours, and had a reputation for being better at laying a siege than preaching.

'You spirited her away from Lusignan, a welcome sight here today.' John's smile was almost a taunt.

Ademar and Alice agreed with him that Isabella was magnificent. The Taillefer family stood proud before John, with Isabella between her parents. She would not escape: her father had stolen her away from the Lusignans and now she would be delivered to the English king.

'And the bishop will bless the wedding tomorrow. You have a very fine cathedral, I believe.'

'Yes, we will make our way there in the morning.'

'Because after the ceremony we must depart almost immediately for Chinon. I have made ready the Archbishop of Bordeaux and several others to sign and witness the marriage and the dowry lands I intend to make as gifts. My mother, too – we will visit her as we travel to Chinon.'

'And Lusignan?' Alice asked. 'You will pass very close to Lusignan as you make your way north.'

John indicated his men, a constant reminder of his strength, but agreed that he would need some assistance skirting any Lusignan lands. 'Peter des Roches is installed in Poitiers now and he has spoken to the mayor there, who has promised that we will be able to make the journey safely.'

Peter des Roches had indeed spoken to the mayor, and others who were eager to work their way into the circle around John.

'The king makes plans, many plans, and some are not as rational and as wise as we would like,' he grumbled to de Mauley, a Poitevin who was a kinsman of the mayor and knew many who would help the Count of Angoulême against the Lusignans.

De Mauley considered, hunched inside his cloak. 'He needs good advisors I think, men with local knowledge and loyalties. Best to make sure he is obeyed and all his plans carried out.'

And they sent out messages, threats and warnings to the small fiefdoms that scattered across the route past Lusignan.

Des Roches smiled as he remembered and signalled to Ademar, who reluctantly joined him at a window, and gave him some news that might or might not please him.

'I believe Oliver de Bonneville and Geoffroy de Bonneville are to accompany John back to England. Their father has sworn them over to John to be young knights of his retinue. They are kinsmen of yours?'

'Indeed, keen young men. Their father must be full of pride.' Ademar stared down at the river; he too was full of pride.

Peter des Roches smiled. 'He has been boasting about it ever since John visited their castle.'

Ademar thought over the news: fellow countrymen to go

with Isabella on her journey to England, and they were close to her in age. This would be a helpful move, and as Agnes would go too, better for all.

John and his group of friends ate with great appetites at the feast that day, a luxurious chaos of dishes, milk, rice, chopped meat and almonds made into sweet white shapes, pork in a sage sauce and a great platter of spiced capon and meatballs. Isabella walked around the table, her head high. She was enjoying the looks and glances from this throng, men who would soon have to acknowledge her as their queen. John grabbed at her arm and pulled her close to him, entranced and delighted with her spirit. She swept away from him with her mother following – tomorrow was the wedding, not tonight.

Peter des Roches laughed at John's grim face. 'She will be yours soon enough. Your lust is still healthy – a good thing after ten barren years with that other queen, that other wife.'

In the chamber above the hall and courtyard, Isabella sat with Agnes and her maids, all known to her from when she lived here as a young child. Gossip was busy and entertaining, and the news of the Bonnevilles' attachment to the retinue of knights was greeted with delight. Agnes was teased about finding a husband in England, or finding one on the journey north, or indeed finding one in the midst of the king's men.

'Oliver is the best horseman in the Angoumois, skilled and strong. We will miss him when he leaves here.'

'He will be a true knight – his brother too.'

Isabella smiled and yawned – it was time these chattering girls left. She dismissed them, haughty and impatient. Away they sped, some calling back to Isabella, jokes and remarks full of innuendo for her future. She frowned; this was not the way to treat a future queen.

'Agnes, help prepare me for bed.'

Agnes closed the chamber door, unlacing the back of Isabella's dress, folding the glorious red and gold silk into the large chest. Tomorrow Isabella would wear the blue gown, the splendid blue and silver fabric showing wealth and also loyalty. If red and gold had shown the power and wealth of the Taillefers, then the blue would mark their obedience and fealty.

Early the next morning Agnes was busy preparing a scented bath. Precious rose oil, drop by drop, turned the hot water cloudy. And then she was busy mixing the rosemary wash for Isabella's hair. She would wear her hair loose today, and her small gold guirland.

Isabella woke up and saw Agnes looking at her, long and thoughtful, ready to make her stir, but she was already throwing back the covers and standing and stretching. Agnes nodded and together they moved to the bath, and Isabella slipped into the milky, perfumed water and rubbed the rosemary wash into her hair. She felt the water running down her back and shivered. Then she was being briskly dried by Agnes, who was determined to treat Isabella to the most thorough of preparations.

Alice entered the room and the three of them unfolded the wedding gown and dressed Isabella. Her chemise was soft and light, the dress heavy and cumbersome. Arranged within it, held within it as if caged, her face pale but proud, she moved to the window and looked down onto a courtyard full of people, horses, carts and wagons. A procession was moving through the crowd, with a stately canon and an even more stately bishop in the centre. The clergy were intent on their walk to the cathedral. Isabella clutched Agnes in a sudden fear. Then she rested her head on the window and took a deep breath. It was her wedding day.

The mass of people thronged about the entrance to the

cathedral, some taking in the carvings around the door: hunting scenes alongside the blessed and the damned, and the brave cavalry charge of Roland at Roncesvalles. The great wealth of Angoulême was the reason for this building, finished three decades ago, and a triumph of stone to match the castle on the hill.

From the castle with its two towers came Isabella, walking slowly, her blue dress moving weightily around her.

John stood in the warm morning sunshine, still for a moment before speaking quietly to the captain of his guards.

'Make sure you have all arms ready, you and the men. If there is trouble I want to be prepared.'

Then he took Isabella's small, pale, bare hand, and placed it over his black-gloved fist, and they made their way through the crowd who quickly stood aside. Alice and Ademar followed, Agnes a little way after them.

'Marry me to this woman, make her my wife.'

The Archbishop trembled slightly as he looked at John, at the rough circle of armed men. He was not sure in his own mind if this was legal. Was John really divorced from that wife back in England? Was Isabella not legally and in every other way betrothed to Hugh Lusignan – in fact had the betrothal not taken place here, before this altar? But he realised very quickly that to resist this command was useless.

'What are we waiting for?'

The words were stammered, the ceremony rapid and finished with haste.

Ademar whispered to Alice as they left the cathedral and began the walk back.

'He has given me La Marche in gratitude for Isabella.'

Alice stopped and gripped his arm. 'La Marche? For you? For us?'

She was astounded: this was welcome news, but danger-ous too. The Lusignans would have humiliation and insult in such depth now, that their call to arms or a call for jus-tice would be difficult for any to ignore. Alice was keenly aware of the feelings that ran through all the local fiefdoms and counties; many thought that the House of Taillefer, the Count of Angoulême and his family, had become full of over-weening pride and ambition. Now they had given Isabella to the King of England, declared for the new ruler, now they had decided where their interests lay, ignoring Philippe of France. She considered the decisions made – there could be no turning away now. They would have to live with the con-sequences.

'Time to feast, husband, and to celebrate, to show the city some joy, to provide a sumptuous show for all to see. Let all Poitevins see how we can provide a holiday.'

The feasting was long and the local wine poured gener-ously. Throngs of people, noisy and greedy, filled the great hall.

Agnes and her father stood together, both anxious about the ride north. Agnes had said goodbye to her mother after the wedding ceremony – she knew that Emma would not want to come to the castle. Too many people worried her. Agnes' father was explaining his trade arrangements to de Bonneville: he wanted this man to know that Agnes was a young woman from a good solid family, and that she would be worth keeping an eye on – it would be useful to have friends from home, from the Poitevin, when they were in London. He had already looked appraisingly at Oliver and Geoffroy. Yes, they were of good stock and loyal, he hoped, to Angoulême.

'How long before they reach the coast?' De Bonneville hoped this merchant with his talk of ships and routes and cargo would know something about the plans that were being made.

'At least twenty days, but they are to stop in Chinon

– dowries to be witnessed and signatures needed. I believe Eleanor is to be visited: she will need to see the new queen. Another young woman from Aquitaine – her approval will assure the marriage.'

'But not yet crowned. First a wedding, then a coronation.'

John was impatient; they would need to leave Angoulême tomorrow or the next day at the latest. He had gifts for Isabella: lands, towns; all these made good dowries. He dismissed thoughts of how some gifts given to Isabella would anger others. But he needed to give her something now, something to mark today. Isabella needed to be decorated and decked with finery and jewels – a queen must look rich.

Among his treasures he found a simple gold collar, the metal slightly beaten to give it texture. He stalked towards her in the chamber high above the river, where she was dancing slowly around the space by the fireplace, making dips and turns in her new lily-embroidered chemise. She had drunk wine and eaten sparingly, her mind a confusion of thoughts: she had been betrothed to Hugh and now she was married to John, and that marriage meant she must live in England, be at his side, be his queen. What did it mean to be married? What did it mean to be a queen? She swayed slightly as she circled. She could hear the music below, pipes and violas joined by lute players. She knew that the crowd was still feasting, dancing and laughing. Why was she up here, away from her parents and friends? Where was Agnes? They had all been here helping her take off the heavy dress, folding it away and scattering rose petals on the bed. There had been jokes and whispers. Why had they gone away and left her to dance alone?

John's face was warm with wine, happy looking at his new bride, happy to slip the collar around her neck. 'Is that enjoyable, the feel of gold – so smooth for such a soft young girl? You didn't resist this marriage, did you, Isabella? You knew you must marry me – you have ambitions like Ademar, like Alice, you knew that the Lusignan alliance was not for you as soon as you saw me in that great hall, and I knew that I must have you.'

He stroked her face above the collar, and her body below it. Isabella trembled and remembered how he had touched her when he met her in the forest, how he had forced the dairy girl that evening in Lusignan.

John held her tight, pressing on her, tickling and stroking around the collar now, pushing her hair away from face, kissing her, whispering what was going to happen, here, now, in this chamber, and then he unfastened the collar and threw it across the room as he tumbled her into the bed.

In the morning Agnes found the collar in the corner and put it away in the small chest, where it rubbed up against silver belts and bronze buckles. Bunches of lavender and letters, and folded pieces of silk lay under these. The chest that had travelled from Lusignan with them both, the chest that had been made here in Angoulême for Isabella, for her special use, for her precious things, for small secrets, for memories.

VII

Angoulême had woken up to a clatter of horses' hooves, sounding like heavy rain on the soft earth in the castle gardens. John was leaving, taking his men and Isabella with her small retinue north to the Loire. They must skirt Lusignan lands as rapidly as possible, and with help they would soon be secure in Chinon.

Ademar and Alice stood watching as the horses and carts moved off, bumping over the cobbles. Isabella had left so quickly: a hurried embrace, a quick whispered farewell and she was gone, on her way to England for the coronation. Alice stood tall and proud in the gateway until the last cart rumbled down the hill and then walked slowly back to the castle, Ademar grinning beside her, both triumphant.

'The journey will be secure – there are plenty of soldiers and John is fierce with his men.'

Alice nodded; she had no fears for the safe passage of the king's party, no fears that the Lusignans would spring an ambush. They were hoodwinked and defeated.

And indeed the journey was uneventful, neighbouring fiefdoms offering a smooth passage, but it was with some relief that John and Peter des Roches approached Chinon and the chapel there, to give thanks for a successful time in the Poitevin, and a successful departure without being pursued. So far, John's actions had not brought about any reaction from the Lusignans.

St Radegonde's chapel lay quiet as the men knelt briefly to mutter thanks. Its new mural of Eleanor was a potent reminder of her great influence in Aquitaine, and on the lives of her children. John's mind was full of memories, of her speed in riding out to Châlus when Richard was dying and how his brother had ended his earthly days in her arms, and how she had surely persuaded Richard then, as he lay dying, to leave all the kingdom to John.

But there was no doubt that Richard was Eleanor's very dearest son, his body buried at the feet of his father in Fontevraud. His heart had been taken from his chest and prepared with frankincense and herbs, embalmed and entombed in the cathedral at Rouen, the Norman capital and a symbol of the strength of the Angevins. And back here, near her own heartlands, in the abbey at Fontevraud, Eleanor mourned him and remembered him.

Last year, John had ridden with haste to Chinon where he had rapidly claimed and taken possession of the royal treasure chests. Next he had ridden to Fontevraud, where he had hammered on the door of the abbey, demanding to pay his respects to his brother's tomb. Finally, and oh so slowly for an impatient man, he had been given permission and escorted to those two tombs, his father's and his brother's. He was escorted by a bishop who refused to join the royal household now that John was king; Bishop Hugh of Lincoln, with his doubts about the succession and Henry and Eleanor's marriage. What a nonsense that was – and almost as much of a nonsense to have to listen to that bishop preaching long sermons.

'By Christ's heels, send a message to this holy man and

tell him that my stomach growls,' John had ordered, not once but three times, famished and irritable, glaring at the man, but he had been ignored.

And then to be lectured about not receiving Holy Communion on Easter Sunday, to be shown sculptures of The Last Judgement and be lectured again. John had pointed at the damned being dragged to Hell.

'Show me rather those, whose good example I mean to follow.'

'You have sworn against religion. An impious prince and king is a scandal.'

John shook his head as he remembered, pulling at his beard and scoffing to himself, staring hard at the painting of his mother. Tomorrow they would ride to Fontevraud to visit her and discuss dowries for Isabella. He had much to tell her and to show her.

He hurried back to Isabella, sprawled in their chamber, tired after the ride and sleepy, her arms stretched above her head. She hardly moved as he slipped an arm around her and carried her to the bed.

Agnes moved out of the room, closing the door behind her, and sat on a stool nearby to await orders, requests, to be a comforting shoulder and presence when all about was so confused and fast-moving. Was it always like this: the hurried departures, the restless visits? She folded her hands in her lap and leant against the wall, waiting quietly. Somewhere a harp and a lute began to play, and the words of a song drifted through the windows high in the walls: *...it seems to me that I felt a breeze from Paradise for love of the lady.*

Eleanor received them in her peaceful abbey where she was attended by her clerks and her chaplain, and her maid. Fontevraud had always been the favoured retreat for aristocratic ladies. They had apartments of their own, away from the monks, nuns, priest and lay brethren, apartments that provided comforts brought from the outside world, but with an air of spiritual comfort too. She was pleased with Isabella, pleased with this smooth-faced girl, her long hair spread down her back, but her spirited, lively eyes only on John. Eyes that seemed to seek her son at every turn, to watch his movements but not to shrink when he passed close to her. Good – she was not scared of him, as others had been. Wary but not scared.

John looked about him. Here he had spent five years from the age of three, some said dumped by his mother, along with his youngest sister. Not wanted or needed by that quarrelling family, but eventually his father had returned to take him back to England and he had learnt to ride alongside his brothers.

Eleanor insisted that they visit the chapel and pray for a safe journey and eventual crossing to England. John knelt beside her. She had always seemed powerful to him, and as he prayed, he thanked God for his mother, who had so ably supported him since he came to the throne. She stood up, a little unsteady now, and Isabella took her arm, holding on tight to this imperious but frail old woman.

'You will give her dowries?' Eleanor walked slowly, glad of Isabella's help, even daring to lean a little for Isabella was as tall as she was, tall indeed for her age.

'I would like to give her Niort and Saintes.' John looked enquiringly at Eleanor. These were her towns – in theory they owned them jointly but he knew that any Aquitaine possession was very dear to her.

'Ah yes, my territories, my inheritance – always uppermost in my thoughts.' She sighed heavily. 'And once so close to being swallowed up into the larger Angevin territory. Your father had many desires: women, land, power. But you know I always wanted Aquitaine to remain mine, and mine alone.

Not so important now that I cannot think to give them to your wife, the new queen.'

'I thought to these we could add Château-du-Loir, Saumur too – generous lands come with these in Poitou: the Saintonge and Anjou. She will have Angoulême and the Angoumois lands in her own right. She is an heiress, as you know.'

'Indeed, she has some inheritance to look to in the future, and this marriage has stopped a dangerous alliance for you, for *us*.' Eleanor smiled at her son as they reached the door to her quarters. 'But I hear that some think it an unprovoked act of dishonour. It is called an act of larceny.'

'By whom?' John flushed, red and angry, his temper breaking, 'Tell me who? I will not have people talking like this – tell me who, I need to know who is being so untrustworthy.'

Eleanor stood away from him and Isabella and looked at them both. 'To some it was ugly news, to others, lovely – you must know that, all will gossip about such a marriage. A little thing, stolen by her father, married to a man so many years older – I know, I know.' She put a hand on John's arm as he began to swear. 'But there will be talk. It might have been more decorous to wait. However, she is entrancing, I can see that, and you have your parents' passions and she has her parents' ambitions. Passion and policy harnessed together.' She beckoned John to bend towards her and whispered in his ear, 'A good and healthy lust, no doubt, to provide you with heirs and me with a grandson or two.'

Her ladies came forward from her rooms, tutting and chiding, and escorted her to a chair. Eleanor sat and gazed at John, a clear-eyed look from a woman and mother who had no illusion about this youngest son, favourite of his father, frequently despised by her. She was still important to him, she thought, and it would all be so very different when she died. She hoped Isabella could wield some power over this cunning, bad-tempered, blasphemous man.

He came forward now and kissed her cheek, bidding her farewell. Isabella followed, curtseying low.

Eleanor placed a hand on her head and murmured, 'Little pawn, I wonder where the game will take you?'

Documents were signed, witnessed. Chinon was full of a swirl of churchmen: the Archbishop of Bordeaux and the several bishops from Aquitaine, Limoges, Périgueux and Saintes, and abbots from Saint-Cybard. John stalked about the writing room, peering at the documents and deciding which signature would suit his purpose best. Isabella listened to all the fine words about how she would be provided for, if widowed, and recited the names of the towns carefully. She was impressed with these, and now knew how important it was to be both an heiress and a queen with named dowry lands and gold.

Agnes combed her hair and helped her dress for the dinner that was to be held for the archbishop and bishops. A frugal meal, that was the order from John – these churchmen did not approve of hearty food.

'Eleanor has this formidable look about her, stern and fierce. She too had important lands that meant much to the men she married: two kings, Agnes!'

'A good wife for both, I am sure. See the influence she has still.'

'And all of this will come to John one day. How wonderful it will be to be Duchess of Aquitaine, such riches!'

Agnes watched her as she made her way down to Chinon's great hall, and remembered that recitation of titles that Isabella had been so proud of when at Lusignan. Well, Queen of England, Duchess of Normandy and Duchess of Aquitaine were certainly a triumphant pinnacle compared with those.

She followed and found Oliver de Bonneville in the corridor. His smile lifted her spirits, and she had noticed that he had begun to linger near the cloisters as if waiting for her to appear.

'Shall we go to eat? It will be a good meal but not over-rich: fish from the river and vegetables in wine and butter.'

Agnes walked as quickly as Oliver; he touched her arm and took his hand away quickly when she looked at it.

'My father is not happy that the cloth is mauled about before being bought.'

'I would not maul, Agnes, I merely wanted to slow you down. We have a long ride ahead – is it possible that we can amble together?'

Agnes glanced sideways and pressed her lips into a tight line. So this was the way it was to go. Well, the riding would be tiring and she was very nervous about the sea journey. A strong arm might be a useful shield.

'Tell me about your home.'

And together they entered the hall in a newfound companionable way, and sat to eat.

Cherbourg and Barfleur were several leagues north of the travellers now, the king riding hard among the knot of men while Isabella and Agnes were placed in the middle of the line for protection, the de Bonneville brothers riding alongside and behind them. The wagons and packs rumbled along, and all were feeling tired at the end of the journey, indifferent to the impatience in the air as John called out, 'Keep together, we need to be together.' His own horse was tiring, and this angered him. He scowled at the group and shouted again.

They had left a large manor house early that morning. Breakfast had been gruel, with salt and butter stirred into the bowls. It had been a hasty night stop and later today they would reach the sea. Isabella and Agnes were secretly scared of what that might look like, and Oliver and Geoffroy knew nothing. Isabella had asked John in the night as they lay together in the hastily arranged chamber, small and cramped but with a good bed, vacated by the lord of the manor and his wife. Their hosts had been nervous about everything, but had managed to feed the king's hungry entourage with spit-roasted pork and baked apples, and then been glad to give up their room and creep away to a safe corner of the hall.

'What is the sea like?'

John was winding her hair around his hands, feeling its weight and letting it drop, as if measuring a fleece just shorn. 'It is deep and dark and it moves all the time, as if it were something alive.' And then he had moved and stretched himself over her, reaching for her hands so that she could not turn away.

They rode all day along the centre of a long, narrow track with high hedges and small fields. There was a tang of salt in the air, and as they neared Cherbourg there were birds wheeling and crying above them, unfamiliar birds with white and grey plumage and big curved beaks. A man who was in charge of one of the wagons said these birds could swim as well as they could fly, and that they caught fish. As they rode on the sun began to set and the town opened up in front of them.

'Oliver, have you understood these people? The family where we stayed last night spoke so strangely, I found myself lost with even the simple words.' Agnes was worried – they were not yet in England and people were already odd in tongue and dress.

'They speak the Norman. It is different, true enough, and our Poitevin is difficult for them.'

John led the weary procession to the big abbey, built by Matilda half a century before and still work continued; a new refectory and chapter house were being added.

'They have a good kitchen and pantry,' Geoffroy told Agnes as rooms were found for them all. 'We will eat and rest well tonight. There is a guesthouse for the soldiers – better than the barns and fields of last night.'

'That is some comfort.' And Agnes helped Isabella through

to the cloister garth where they sat quietly and rested on the grass-topped bench. An arbour closed one side of the garth from the sun and late roses bloomed all along its edge. After the dusty ride this was peace indeed.

In the morning the wind was blowing from the northeast so no sea journey was possible. The ships were waiting next to a simple harbour wall built of local granite, men were checking stores and bundles and there were canvas slings being readied to get the horses on board.

'I will be busy with plans for the crossing all day. Take Agnes and one or two young knights and pray for a safe journey at the chapel near the harbour.' John ran his hands down Isabella's back as he spoke, nuzzling her neck.

She leant against him briefly. He never seemed to tire of touching her, it was incessant; indeed, a few hours without his restless caresses would be welcome. She turned and watched him leave. It was strange indeed, this marriage to a king, but he had primed her full of talk of the coronation and the gifts he would lay at her feet, and so she would pray for a safe voyage.

The chapel of St Germain perched on the harbour was over two hundred years old, built small and low against the cold winds, but close to the shore. Today the heavy granite blocks were warm to the touch as Isabella and Agnes entered its simple space. They walked to the front and knelt to pray on the stone floor. There were painted walls and a carving of a cross on one of the stones.

'My lady, I would speak with you.' An elderly priest stood at the door, blocking the light. He held out his hand, which held a great, golden, tawny lump, rough like a rock on one side, smooth and glowing on the other. 'This is amber – it was brought here by the Norsemen, more than five hundred years ago, when they raided the coast. They buried it in the ground, just here, wrapped in a cloth. We found it when we made the new path to the beach. Here, hold it – it is almost a living thing.'

Isabella took the amber and felt the rough underside and the smooth dome. She heard the priest telling Agnes about the founding of the chapel and its importance to the local people.

'There was a Christian building here long ago. We have always had a place of worship close to the sea, for from the sea came the Norsemen with their long ships and their cruelty, but our town was the town of the church. The church was threatened too, but it was here before they came, and it has stood here for centuries. They could smash and raid but we always had the church.'

His words reminded Isabella of stories about her own family and Angoulême – on a river, not on the sea, but her Taillefer family had built a wooden fort on the rocks and defended the land against the men who came up the river. She knew about war and attack and defence from these stories, and the importance of holding onto what was yours.

'The first Count of Angoulême fought these men too, he was a most strong knight, a magnificent man, and he built churches like this one. He killed one of the kings of the Norsemen, and was himself killed in that battle. Our region was captured and burned, but now we flourish.'

Isabella handed back the amber, and the priest blessed her and said softly as she moved away, 'Be always careful and remember this piece, how rough and how smooth it is all in one. That is how people can be too.'

Agnes hurried to keep up with Isabella as she reached the path to the town. The de Bonnevilles were waiting and looked worried as the two rushed past them.

'What is the matter? Isabella, wait for me – slow down, you may well stumble on this rocky path.'

'I will not stumble, I will not be attacked and defeated. I must remember who I am, a Taillefer who is to be crowned Queen of England. Surely there will be a place for me where I can be someone who knows power? The king has me in his bed and I will have power.'

Agnes soothed and counselled as they walked more slowly, thinking that Isabella, so recently a difficult child, still learning to embroider and sew, was now changed, and still changing. She sighed after the old life, known and understood, and as they headed over the rise in the path she saw the seaport and the ships, waiting to take them to their new life in a new country.

VIII

Isabella and John crossed the sea, leaving Barfleur, their ship, the royal galley, long, low and slim. It was a speedy crossing with a good following wind, and the sailors said that the autumn gales would begin soon, that all were lucky to have the best sailing weather. John smiled at this and held onto Isabella's arm, as they stood and watched the waves. She turned to shelter in his embrace. It was the first time she had seen such water, not rapid and deep like the Charente, the long river near her home, but wide, swelling and falling, and the ship cutting through the swell, always going forward, its dragon prow surging. The other vessels, full of men and horses and household goods, rode the waves alongside.

Isabella looked for Agnes, but she suffered from the sea malady and spent her time below.

'I hope you will revive on land – I would need your help for the coronation. John has planned this for soon – very soon – after we arrive. I am to be anointed and crowned, his queen and wife.'

Agnes turned away and retched.

Isabella put out a hand and touched her shoulder. 'The wind drives us on to Portsmouth, do not despair. Soon we will be riding to London.'

London was big and bustling, and Isabella's eyes were always on John as they approached through the narrow, crowded streets. He had vowed never to leave her side. She was not sure if she was comforted by his words or made uneasy by them.

Indeed, thought Agnes sourly, as Isabella had told her this; indeed, he stays with you night and day. She listened wearily as Isabella told her all she knew about this great city.

'Agnes, we are to stay in the Palace of Westminster, the royal palace – such a place! It is built on the Eyot of Thorns, is that not a strange name? I am told it is a small island where the River Tyburn joins the Thames. A palace built by the river. A river that will remind me of home.'

Agnes walked quickly through the rooms that led one to the other in the palace at Westminster. She was still unsure about her way around the passages. The queen's chamber overlooked a courtyard and the king's chamber overlooked the river, she knew this, but it all seemed so circular. Her eyes were downcast and her hands twisted at the blue cloth of her skirt, her nails bitten and ragged. She almost bumped into a man walking towards her. He put out a hand to steady her as she flushed and bobbed her head.

'By the bells of Hell, take care where you put your feet,' he growled. And unfriendly, he strode away.

Agnes took a deep breath and thought longingly of home where she could be herself, not like the position she found herself in now. Attempting to please everyone, trying to follow orders that made little sense, and always seemingly wrong. But at last she was at the door of the rooms where Isabella slept, and although the place was full of others, all rushing about and trying to help and getting in the way of the preparations for the coronation, Agnes felt pleased to see that Isabella was receiving so much attention.

'A present from the King,' whispered one lady, bundling cloaks into Agnes' arms. 'Can you find a chest to store them?'

Agnes folded away the three cloaks, one of scarlet wool, two of linen. There was a heavy fur pelisse as well and Agnes admired the soft grey warmth of this – it would be wanted in an English winter. Isabella's wardrobe was becoming sumptuous. But John's gift to Isabella was not that generous, she thought as she closed the chest. True, he had given her a crown of pearls and rubies and very fine it was, with filigree work and the seven points also set with jewels. But Agnes knew that John himself had such a magnificent collection of jewels, all of great worth and excellence. She knew his clothes were magnificent too, and that he constantly sought out the best materials. She had noticed the sapphires sewn onto his gloves – he was very acquisitive, she thought, and greedy.

Isabella was finally ready to walk to the abbey. She had four great ladies to accompany her and John would meet her at the door. Agnes sighed as she watched the small group slowly move away from the king's palace. It would have been a great thing to see her crowned, but she must stay here and make the chamber ready again.

The candles and tapers flickered through the huge grey abbey, dedicated to St Peter, built close to the Thames. It had not been far for Isabella to walk to the church that Londoners called the west minster.

Long before she arrived the choristers had moved into place. Their gowns were fusty and sombre and disappeared into the gloom of the choir stalls. These were deeply carved with strange beasts: some like dragons; others were men with trailing leaves about their faces and still more were grinning bearded infidels. The choir moved quietly along the rows and waited for the arrival of the king and queen. The tapestries that were used to decorate the choir were in place today, a proud gift of English cloth and arras work. The choir settled, glad of the mercy seats that would help them rest through the long ceremony.

As Isabella arrived there had been a surge of movement at the entrance. People began to move and jostle as now the bishops, abbots and large groups of clergy, all wearing their silken hoods, escorted John and Isabella as far as the choir. A solemn procession: men carrying tapers, censers, holy water; a mass of colour, light and song, the choir chanting triumphal praise. There were barons, earls and knights, all mixed in with clergy, and there was William Marshall, the man who had supported John from the very beginning. He and some of the other men took Isabella to the high altar. The Archbishop of Canterbury, Hubert Walter, moved towards her, praying to Almighty and everlasting God, the fountain of all truth. John stood to one side, his crown fixed low on his forehead, watching. A second coronation for him.

Isabella's long train, with its gold and silver woven into patterns of lilies and lions, swept the flagstones. She bowed her bare head, and all her long hair hung loose about her face as she knelt. She could feel the herbs and rushes strewn over the floor. She knew a man had been paid many shillings to provide these.

The Archbishop made a simple blessing, 'May the anointing of this oil increase you in your office and strengthen you forever.'

She had knelt as she had been told because unction was to be given, the holy oil anointing her breast and her head, anointing her as queen consort, a twice anointed queen. 'Pour your divine spirit over this handmaiden, may she remain worthy and chosen, strong and steadfast.'

The silvery-gold spoon that held the oil was glinting, and she could see the four pearls that decorated the stem. The oil smelt of roses and cinnamon bark. The Archbishop of

Canterbury was praying fervently for her prudent counsel and virtue, and no doubt for her fertility too, she thought as she kept still and quiet on the stone floor.

'Receive the ring of Faith.'

A gold ring with a large square ruby surrounded by sixteen small rubies, all dull, almost black, but somewhere deep inside, fire.

'Receive the crown of glory and the office of joy.'

And then they were singing the hymn, the singing paid for by the chamberlains of the Norman exchequer. Orders came: pay the chaplain and the songster twenty-five shillings for singing *Christus Vincit* at the unction and crowning of the lady queen. And John was happy to pay for this, and for her crown which had been put in place, a circle of gold with pearls and rubies, not heavy but tight. More simple chanting, sweet singing in the choir, censers releasing their spice and perfume. Then it was time to stand again, and be turned around to where John waited for her, his face thoughtful in the watery light from the weak October sunshine as it lit up the glorious stained glass windows. The Mass was sung, gold was offered, and Archbishop Hubert led John and Isabella back through the crowds, people all around exclaiming that she was now Queen of England. The monks would write that Isabella of Angoulême was crowned queen by the common consent of the barons, clergy and people of England.

And then they went to dine, all the tables full, the kitchens busy, the serving frantic as the clamour grew for wine.

'What are you thinking, John?'

Hubert Walter had crowned John the previous year on Ascension Day, making sure that his right to be king was assured by the people. He had stressed that John was elected king by his brother and stopped any muttering about the nephew, Arthur, and his hereditary claims.

'About my brother's coronation and its bad omen.'

'The bat that flew overhead in the middle of the day? Yes, that was a sign of woes to come.'

'But today is a good day, a Sunday to rejoice.' John threw a careless arm around Isabella. 'We have crowned this Isabella our queen, to share the royal power, and we will make sure we mark this day with much pleasure.'

Restless as always, John took the court away from London, determined to visit his inheritance and explore who was likely to be loyal and who was not. He was eager to hunt too, and there was no finer place for that than Savernake Forest, close by to Marlborough Castle, the great castle given to him by Richard. Isabella and Agnes rode in the middle of the train of horses and men, the de Bonnevilles riding with them. A welcome escort, for they had hardly seen them since their arrival in England.

The autumn winds were nipping at everyone as they saw the castle and its keep high on the small hill.

'Seven towers,' Geoffroy de Bonneville said admiringly as they crossed the drawbridge and found the inner courtyard full of servants and grooms ready to stable the horses.

Agnes was shown where to find the queen's chamber, beyond the chapel and the great hall, and looked around in dismay. Everything was rough stone, no scented herbs were strewn on the floor, and there were very few candles and a great lack of tapestries to soften the walls. The bed was narrow and the rope base needed attention. She set a grim face to the tasks of unpacking the chests and wondered if anyone had ever considered the young queen in this place.

'They say that Merlin's bones are somewhere here, wise Merlin who knew who was treacherous and who was the king's friend.' John walked Isabella to the north inner gate and indicated the steep steps that gripped the side of the hill; a long climb up to the keep. 'The view from the keep is long and wide – you will be able to watch me set out and return from the hunt. We will be gone all day, from sunrise to sundown, many fine fat deer to chase. I like Marlborough; a well-fortified castle, but it has not seen much fighting, so I think it is a safe place to leave you while I journey north and east. I must go to the Welsh Marches and to Lincoln.'

He caught her around the waist and tipped her face towards him. 'Well, my little queen, will you be safe here without me?'

'But I am with you always, night and day. We are never parted, why must I stay here now, in this place far from London and you riding out to the hunt or riding away north?' She scowled at him and tried to escape his hands.

John held her tighter and whispered, 'Day and night, night and day, when we eat and drink, before we sleep and when we wake all I want is to be with you, and I will be with you again and again. And my queen, how we sleep after such times together, a sleep that is like magic to me. Have you cast a spell on this king?' He kissed her face, her angry face, and pulled her closer to him. 'And now, after the journey, to bed I think.' And he almost dragged her away from the wide gate and towards the buildings.

Some days began at dawn, early for hunting, and finished late with feasting and gambling; some days began late because John would not leave the bedchamber, would not leave Isabella until the sun rose high.

An order for a tun of wine arrived and it was rolled into the cellars, and flagons brought up to the great hall. Here it was drunk down as the king gambled, insisting that Oliver and Geoffroy join him in games of dice.

'It is a lucky thing that the King has a royal mint here,' grumbled Oliver to Agnes as they walked in the cloisters, pleased to find themselves with some time to talk after the week of non-stop entertainment.

'And I hear there is treasure stashed away too, he must trust and like this castle indeed.'

'You will be looked after while he travels, Agnes: there are many counsellors using the castle, and clerks writing all the time. The forest has men working here on those accounts, too – John likes to watch carefully all those figures, expenses, purchases, even if he does throw dice about.'

Agnes smiled; it was warming to hear someone worry about her and reassure her. She had been glad to leave London and the great ladies who spoke too quickly and gave orders too roughly. She thought about Isabella, and decided to confide in Oliver.

'The queen, she is being accused by some of witchcraft, in the way that John stays with her till midday. Their chamber is a place of indolence and the bed is never empty.'

'Except when he is playing dice! I think he would take her to the hall in her night chemise and dandle her on his lap if he could, but she would distract him from the game.'

'And others are whispering that they do not go to the chapel and pray. Isabella seems to have forgotten all the piety she was taught.'

Oliver stopped and spoke very seriously to Agnes, his words careful and measured. 'Agnes, we speak of Queen Isabella and King John but we must keep ourselves out of gossip's harm too, and I would not want your name dragged about with mine.' He took her hand and spoke again. 'I want to be true to you when I travel away, and will hope your heart is true to mine.'

'It is, Oliver, and we will remember each other for today and all the days to come.'

A long, loving embrace and then they turned and walked back to the courtyard.

*

Marlborough Castle was quiet again; the horses and men had left for Gloucester, with John shouting orders and galloping ahead. Agnes sorted out clothes and bed linen for the washerwomen, while Isabella sulked and kicked at the chests, fiddling with the locks and sighing, and then threw on the grey fur cloak that John had given her on her coronation day and flung out of the room.

She thought about climbing up to the top of the keep. She had done this one morning when the hunt left and it had been exhilarating standing at the top of the mount, feeling as if she could open her arms and fly across the small town and into the forest. But her mood today was too sour to take any joy in doing that, and she stomped along the cloister and turned into the chapel.

A rose window glowed at the far end and the candles near the altar had been lit. Isabella walked towards the light, remembering the prayer she had been taught. *Angel of God, my guardian dear, to whom his love commits me here; ever this day, be at my side, to light and guard, to rule and guide. Amen.* She could say it now and she could say it in the night too, *ever this night*, and perhaps it would help her as seeing the amber in Cherbourg had helped her to decide to be strong and to win some power for herself. Well, she had been in the king's bed for weeks now and her power was still there, but had she gained anything for herself? A coronation, that was true, and those lands John had promised her in Poitou. She pulled the cloak more closely. She had been given these clothes too, but John had jewels and finery beyond all this and he showed no sign of giving her more. Her sulky anger bubbled away as she began to leave.

An elderly, bent-over man busy trimming some candles in the porch straightened up with a creaky groan. 'My lady, the queen, crowned in London – more than Avisa, greater than Avisa, but he has brought you back to Marlborough where he married that first wife.'

*

Isabella raged at Agnes, her tears and sobs distorting the angry words.

'He married Avisa here, that wife he so easily put aside, but he has brought me back to the same place where he married her, took her to bed. I will not think about it, I will not dwell on it.'

'Hush, hush, we will not be here forever. Oliver tells me that we are to leave for London and spend the feast of Christmas south of there in a manor house, close by one of the many royal hunting lodges. There is a great forest called Windsor.'

Isabella flung herself down onto the bed. 'I am tired of the hunting, always hunting and playing cards, and visiting his people and the towns and the bishops, and nothing for me. Nothing for me – I am the anointed queen, I am called vice-regent, but I have nothing. I am turned into nothing. You are fortunate to have a friend and companion in de Bonneville. The king is not my friend.'

Angry tears and hot words, thought Agnes; this is not what is wanted or needed. She threw a wool blanket over Isabella and soothed her to sleep.

IX

Guildford, Christmas 1200
Canterbury, Easter 1201

The manor house at Guildford had been made ready, and the steward ordered the servants to fill the rooms and the hall with yew branches, holly and tall candles. There was a holy bough hanging by the big door, dark green bay, rosemary and box with mistletoe woven through it, and in the centre of the square a Christ child. Isabella and John paused as they stood under it, and were welcomed in.

The gabled buildings were built around a courtyard, and a gatehouse tower with its bridge sat facing towards the old Roman road. Tracks into the woodland snaked out from this. The house and its farm were surrounded by a moat where carp swam deep under the weeds. The deer wandered in, or jumped through the deer-leaps cut into the large bank topped with wooden posts. This held back the forest.

'They are trapped,' said Isabella. 'Trapped so easily.'

'They make good venison, and a haunch will be served on Christmas Day. I hear they make a pie of all the pieces of heart, liver and such, for the villagers to eat for their feast.'

Agnes was enjoying this place. It was more serene than Marlborough, with better accommodation, and she was reluctantly and grudgingly pleased that the king insisted on having a bathtub with him wherever he travelled. And here it was guarded by the special attendant, William Brown, bathman, who was in charge of filling it with hot water. He had carried the water up to the king's chamber and now while John was out, riding to Windsor, it was for Isabella. She rinsed her arms and legs and Agnes scooped water over her head, then helped her from the wooden tub, bundled her into a linen cloth and fetched her chemise and gown.

'You will need your mantle, the one lined with fur. It is beginning to snow.'

It snowed all that Advent. John was more restless than ever as the weather stopped the hunting and he could only throw himself into the feasting and gambling, throwing dice with his retinue, and laughing at their losses. If he wasn't in the great hall he was consulting with the clerk of the household expenses and the butler, checking the stores ordered for the season: the dozen or so hogsheads of wine from Bristol, the several pounds of saffron and almonds, the dried fruit and spices. Isabella trailed after him, Agnes walking behind her.

'You were learning how to do all this,' reminded Agnes. 'You were beginning to keep a tally of goods in Lusignan.'

Isabella rounded on her. 'I am a queen now, it is different.'

But her face spoke differently: she wanted to be in charge of something, wanted to give orders too, but John held her arms behind her back when she began to ask questions, and fondled and kissed her and told her to stop pestering him.

On Christmas Eve he was more indolent. This was his birthday, and he was intent on holding Isabella in bed until noon, his great feather bed heaped with linen sheets, rugs and furs. The heavy hangings in the chamber kept it warm, and the room glowed with firelight.

'There are many gifts to give – I have more than a hundred expecting new robes this winter. And you must have something from me: new linen towels from the mills in Ireland, so fine and soft for you, you who are so rosy and moist after your bath.' He nuzzled at Isabella's neck and wrapped his body around her. 'I enjoy all the pleasures with you. Everything I want is mine.'

Isabella felt faint with the heat of the room, the heavy furs and John's body pushing into her.

He twisted her head to face him and his voice, thick with desire, repeated, 'Everything I want is mine.'

The Christmas Day feasting lasted through three meals. Isabella picked at the woodcock roasted with butter and saffron, while others were tearing into the roast goose and apples. Agnes was spooning up frumenty, thickened with eggs today; she was entranced by the dried fruit and spices which made the porridge so full of flavour. Her face was pink and plump in the candlelight and Oliver squeezed her thigh under the tablecloth. It was good to see her relaxed for a change instead of worrying about Isabella all the time.

John cut rough chunks of bread and cheese, drank great beakers of wine and put his head on the table as the musicians sang.

Heaven and Earth and also Hell,
And all that ever in them dwell,
Of your coming they will behave well,
Good day! Good day, good day,
My lord Sir Christemass, good day!

John growled along with the minstrels, and then signalled for another song. They started up again.

Now to amend, God give us grace,
I have repentance and much space,

In Heaven to see his glorious face,
Where we shall amend and do no wrong.

An irritable roar from the king. 'Sing something more cheerful, more lusty than that! I do not wish to amend and do no wrong – sing of the women and the summer.'

Some be brown and some be white
And some be tender as a tripe,
And some of them be cherry ripe
Yet all they be not so.
Some be lewd, and some be shrewd
We will go where they go.

The great hall was filled with laughter and clapping, some beating their hands on the table. John stood up to bow and strut for them, his red satin cloak magnificently embroidered with sapphires and pearl, his tunic belt and sword belt studded with garnets, diamonds and emeralds. White gloves, pulled off and thrown onto the chair, glowed with rubies.

Isabella knew that many saw her as the ripe cherry, tender and lewd, but she would sit proudly and let them laugh because she knew their king was a restless man. They were not staying here beyond the New Year and she would not have to hear those words, full of mischief, again.

Indeed on New Year's Day, John had ridden north into the winter snows, with Isabella and Agnes bundled up in cloaks and furs, escorted again by the de Bonnevilles.

'I must check, far into the Scottish Marches, and see that all are as loyal as I want. Then to Cumberland, and across the winter road to the east. Everywhere must be surveyed. At Easter we will meet with the archbishop in Canterbury: another place that my father marked.' A harsh laugh, and a relentless stare.

And it was a relentless progress through the north for the court. Candlemas Day was spent in Scarborough Castle. Isabella took delight in ordering pancakes for the meal that evening. It was a reminder of the Feast of Chandeleur in France, when the batter was beaten and whisked and then fried, the golden pancakes reminding all of the sun that would arrive with springtime.

'Dew on Candlemas, winter at its final hour. We used to say that on the second day of February.' Agnes was sifting flour, helping with the preparation. Isabella welcomed the warmth of the castle kitchen; she had cracked eggs and stirred them into a thick mass. A maid stood waiting to pour the batter into a hot skillet. The small domestic pleasures brought them both to memories of home, and an ache of homesickness. But the northeast Yorkshire coast was far from the Poitevin, from Angoulême and its lush countryside.

'No chance of the end of winter here, this coast is the coldest I have known. And such a tower! How far can they see from its great height? It must command the sea.'

'The king's chambers are comfortable, all the knights are pleased to be here. It is good lodging for the court and its retinue.'

'What does Oliver say of the ride here and the business to be conducted? I am told nothing and given no news.' Isabella stared into the fire. Why was she so ignored, not considered worth any explanation? For John she was just something to spoil.

'Wherever he goes the King lays heavy fines on the people, claiming they have laid waste to the royal forests. The money will be used for defences, and this castle is to have some building work. Oliver says that the king cares for it as is so strategic against the north. The barons must be watched.'

Isabella now knew that everywhere her husband suspected

betrayal; he needed to constantly check on loyalties. He was sure of her; he had kept her so close whenever they were together that there was no chance of any idle friendship. Only Agnes was there as a good companion, someone to talk to about home, although John frowned if they were secretive together for too long.

'Always the chance that there will be blabbing,' he would say, scowling and sending Agnes out of the room. His plans now took him even further north, and he ordered Isabella to stay in the castle.

'And you, for you, here is the best place to stay, safe and strong. My father made this place, built it of stone. We know how to build in stone. Henry made Dover Castle too – both that and this castle are great fortresses. Dover has a mighty keep, and such a great tower: the walls as thick as four men standing one on the other. And Dover guards the gateway to England. This castle guards the crossroads to the north, and I will make it splendid, make it such a stronghold with its own great tower. And now it is to keep you as well, all my treasure.'

A last set of instructions to stewards and butlers, a last check that the sack of silver pennies to pay for provisions was locked in the treasury, and a last fierce kiss for Isabella.

Time passed slowly, sitting in that great stone building. Isabella and Agnes watched the sea beating on the shore, looking across the bay. Steep cliffs on three sides, and a sheer drop down to the leaden grey waves.

'Wool is traded from here – it is a busy, thriving port for the English, all going to Calais and beyond. Expensive English wool: good quality but the price is always high.'

Agnes knew about the all-important competition with the marts of the Low Countries; her father travelled there each year to buy wool. And thoughts of her family brought about the truth: they were both still feeling homesick. The de Bonneville brothers had ridden away with John, there was no amusement perched here on top of the cliffs, and the north-east wind blew all the time, making walking in the grounds uncomfortable for them. Isabella listened listlessly to any bits and pieces of news Agnes was able to glean: John had made friends again with his half-brother Geoffrey, Bishop of York; it had snowed for three days on the Northumberland roads and the heavy carts had to crawl along, taking detours to find roads not buried; fine-wooled sheep were now selling for ten pence. It all meant so little to her. She slept late and went to bed early. Bored she might be, but she was glad of the peace.

The cold eased a little as they travelled south, first to London and then to Canterbury. Easter was nearly the end of March, and the spring was late this year. But even the sharp winds that blew across the Channel and bit into the corner of Kent seemed warmer than the constant north-easterlies that had made Yorkshire seem so inhospitable. Near to Canterbury, the old Roman road, the Watling Way, was busy, lined with inns to accommodate the pilgrims who thronged to the city, with many coming by ship from the Continent into Dover, and all intent on visiting the grave of Thomas Becket.

John gripped Isabella's arm as she stared at the floor of the cathedral crypt. A stone cover had been placed over the burial place, with two holes where pilgrims could insert their heads and kiss the tomb.

'My father thought him a low-born clerk, a traitor. They had such disagreements and then the knights murdered him. And now he is a saint and brings a mass of pilgrims to Canterbury. Good for the treasury and for the wellbeing of the town, no doubt.'

'I will just kneel and pray,' Isabella said faintly, and did so. Trinity Chapel was quiet so early in the morning. She held her hands and prayed, but her thoughts were not particularly holy. There was to be an Easter celebration, for they would wear their crowns again and process here for Mass, and then they would return to their private apartments and change the heavy crowns and robes for lighter ones, for the feast that would follow. She wondered if John had ordered her a new gown – it would be pleasing to have another new, fine dress. Dark red wool would look pretty in candlelight.

Hubert Walter, Archbishop of Canterbury and chancellor, a man happy in holding both the high ecclesiastical office and the high secular office, had begun work on the Archbishop's Palace. It was an expensive undertaking as all about was decay and semi-ruin. He was laying the foundations of the hall and planning two decorated gateways, one for porters and tradesmen and one near the cathedral. A square tower was being sketched and drawn; the cloisters and a green court were already built.

John strode about the work, making rough estimates of costs. Was Hubert borrowing to make this sumptuous place? John knew about building costs – had he not just left Scarborough where he had spent money, several hundred pounds, and was planning to spend more? Good work was dear.

Hubert was indeed a fine administrator, the best that John could hope for; he had asked him to be chancellor as soon as he had the crown. The Pope had made a noise about an archbishop holding this office too, and for a few months Hubert had stepped down, but was soon back again and with such natural authority that most deferred to his judgement. But was he running up debts?

There was knowledge between them; dark knowledge. John's attempt at rebellion against Richard, seventeen years before, had been stopped by Hubert. Richard ransomed, and returning to England.

'The Devil is loose,' the French king had warned, for Philippe and John had plotted together but their letters were intercepted. John's own household cleric, Adam of St Edmunds, his leather pouch full of letters for the keepers of the castles belonging to John, ordering fortifications against Richard's arrival, had visited Hubert in London. There he had eaten dinner with the archbishop and boasted about John's wealth, his prosperity and the close friendship between John and the King of France.

'The French king has given my lord two castles, Driencourt in the north and Arches near the centre, and would give him more if John had faithful men to keep them for him. Is this not proof of a great friendship?'

'Indeed. Well, my good priest, you must be weary after your long journey. I am sure you are anxious to find your lodgings.'

Adam left, with a full belly and a foolish heart, to make his way back to his rooms. Along the way two men pounced, grabbed his arms and he was arrested on the order of the Mayor of London, who took away all his papers and turned them over to the archbishop.

It was easy for the archbishop to show the treasonable letters to the assembled bishops and barons.

'These wicked instructions are preparation for civil war, John's castles against Richard's. We must act swiftly. John's lands in England will be taken from him, his castles seized.'

Rapid agreement from all. Hubert had besieged Marlborough Castle himself and made sure that John was excommunicated; something they both ignored now. It was important to make progress with all the government they planned. Important to be on good terms.

So Hubert had crowned John, making sure that he swore the oath to love the holy church and her ordained priests, to see justice rightly administered throughout England. And had cautioned John not to accept the crown unless he fully intended to keep the oath, because the archbishop had been wary from the beginning of this runt of the Angevin litter; wary enough to make a speech about electing a king from among the family. A speech that emphasised how John's right was based on the importance of being the brother of Richard who had no heirs, on the importance of his royal blood.

'And on this basis he is elected. Hear, all of you, and be it known that no one has an antecedent right to succeed another in the kingship, unless he shall have been unanimously elected.'

There were stories about the Angevin blood, stories that the family laughed about. They were tainted, some said, with devils' blood brought into the family by a beautiful woman, wife to a Count of Anjou, a countess who could not take communion in the Mass and who, when challenged, flew out of a high window of the church. This story was used to explain the temper that gripped Henry II and his sons, John as bad as any, gnawing his fingers and falling to the floor in fits of anger.

And indeed John was working himself into a small petty rage now. He had heard about the Christmas feast at Canterbury, about the celebrations that Hubert had arranged. Clothes had been distributed to those attending.

'I have to resort to some plain words, angry words. Do you wish to put yourself on par with the king?' An abrupt turn as he walked across the building site. 'And these restorations, they cannot be cheap. Your architect seems to make expensive suggestions.'

'It is true I have made elaborate plans for the Archbishop's Palace but with all the pilgrims coming here it needs to be done. The debt will be paid, do not be concerned about that. The Jews will lend for a Christian archbishop's lodging. A nice point, I think. I am beginning a new system to fight against the fraud that exists in that moneylending business. At times both parties make trouble and dissent – the court has no way of knowing the truth but now I have scribes who make copies of all the records of agreements, and these go to the treasury. With the record there can be proper accounting.'

John reached out his hand, a smile replacing the scowl. 'Very good indeed, and are your loans recorded too?'

'I have the greatest help from Jacob, the Jew of Canterbury. He is the leading money man.'

'It is useful that Canterbury has six or seven mints! Plus a rich Jew.'

John was in a good mood again. Money flowing meant that taxes could and would be paid. He liked the treasury to be full.

On Easter Day, clear and bright, Agnes dressed Isabella in her coronation gown and Hubert performed the ceremony of placing the crowns on the heads of John and Isabella. Five bishops thronged around them, and many barons were anxious to see that the king and queen were again in attendance. The archbishop led the procession back to his establishment where the feasting and entertainment arranged for the court was magnificent.

The whispers and the gossip were incessant: such an occasion! The royal court, the archbishop's assembly, many powerful barons, the long tables set with linen cloths, pewter and silver. Candles everywhere, lighting the afternoon's gloom.

'The queen is very young. Beautiful, that is true – some say the Helen of Troy of France. Look how John dotes on her!'

More warm spiced wine was drunk and more small dishes of sweetmeats passed, one to the other, as heads came together for much comment, much murmuring about men who delighted in the beauty of their wives.

'It must be that John has not read those saints, Thomas Aquinas and Jerome, who say that wives are not to be treated as objects of desire, solely for pleasure. A man who is too passionately in love with his wife is like a man with a whore: all caresses, sweet flesh, lascivious kisses and shameful embraces.'

The two noble lords nodded wisely as they agreed how wrong this was. Marriage was for producing children, not enjoying the soft couch with a woman under you.

'She seems to lean towards him and then pull away, but as if it were a game. For one so young she seems lusty indeed. It will be important for England to have heirs from this last son of Henry's. No children from Richard's marriage, and Richard dead, young King Henry dead, Geoffrey, Duke of Brittany dead, his son young and not supported for the crown by Eleanor.'

'That wise old harridan! We will not see her in England again.'

And when the talk was not of Isabella and John, the whispers turned to the feasting and the way that Archbishop Hubert was restoring the palace at Canterbury.

'Look at the money he is spending! The candles alone must have cost over one hundred shillings.'

'Hubert is showing his king a very great display. Too much, some would say.'

And so the months had passed for John since the August marriage and the October coronation, months of business and constant travel mixed with feasting and lustful indolence, and Isabella. Isabella, who was sometimes petulant and child-ish, but still his queen.

And John, a king where none had thought he would be, John Lackland who had turned against all his brothers and his father, his father who loved him more than all his other sons, betrayed on his deathbed by John.

John, elected, crowned, anointed, sitting with old enemies,

constant friends and a new young wife. But trying hard to shake out of his memory the awful prophecy: that the brood of the wicked should not thrive, that the descendants of Henry must bear a curse, and that the French king would entirely destroy the Angevins, the House of Anjou, the dynasty and empire that had mastery of so much.

X

France and England, 1201–1202

Eleanor of Aquitaine, as old and frail as she might be, was still a woman of influence. She was alert to the outside world even in her cloistered life in the abbey and as Easter approached, whispers of gathering trouble had reached her in Fontevraud. Bedridden after a long illness, she sat propped up by pillows as her ladies, trying to keep her quiet and calm, shooed people away from the door. But her instincts were still working, her mind holding onto all hopes for peace in the Poitou. The rumours of war disturbed her and she sent for the Viscount of Thouars, an ally she hoped she could still count on. Before he arrived she called her secretary – there was a need to make decisions and plans. A need to practise Eleanor's diplomacy skills again.

'Aimery is not a strong character, frequently buffeted by fear. His loyalty is always political, always seeking the best side for his own interests.'

Guy nodded. 'True, but his estates are large and he controls the approaches from the north. He is powerful in that respect, and others not so strong in wealth and land will follow him.'

Eleanor sighed. 'John had his help before when he had just inherited the English crown. Aimery was there, attacking Arthur's supporters, and John rewarded him well for this. And then what did he do? He took away the seneschal offices he had given him!'

Guy spoke softly; he did not want to upset the ailing queen. 'It is not John's way to give anything to men he considers powerful, if he can avoid it.'

Eleanor smiled at him; she knew her son well and was not offended. 'He distrusts too much, we both know that. But in the event of any kind of war, now that the Lusignans have woken up to the full extent of the wrong done to them and are becoming turbulent, we must make sure of Aimery.'

Hugh and Ralph sat either side of the table in the great hall at Lusignan. If trouble was looming, it would start here. They were making sure that all knew of how their ambitions had been thwarted. This rankled and festered, as did the great insult done to them by John.

Hugh had been stunned when the news of the theft of Isabella reached him, stunned at the hasty marriage, the loss of the valuable prize that was Isabella. Another dark Angevin insult.

And he was confounded by Ralph who had let her go, let her ride off with her father and her baggage carts and her maid, the whole of Lusignan doffing their caps and saying Godspeed. Godspeed to a father who would sell his daughter to the highest bidder. Isabella, now Queen of England and married to that lecher.

'I waited for her to come of age for marriage – I would not have the girl, not yet thirteen years old, married and in my bed. I had some integrity and he had none. There was a betrothal in front of the bishop in Angoulême Cathedral, we said the words for the future: I will take you as my wife, I will take you as my husband. It was binding and John broke that. It was a deliberate act and her father helped with the deception, he lied through his teeth to me.'

Ralph was still furious and bitter about the story he had swallowed. He had let Isabella go with her father, home to Angoulême and to another husband. For both of them the betrayal by John had been galling. 'Perhaps there would be compensation. There should be some.'

'There will be none – what can he offer us that would be in any way recompense? And everyone saw how powerful he was last year, parading through here. We know while Eleanor lives the Aquitaine will be loyal. But for Lusignans to appear so subdued by that Softsword, it ill becomes us!'

'We are not cowards, Hugh. The Lusignans are not cowards.'

But they had sworn allegiance to John; even if it was an allegiance they no longer wished to keep. An allegiance made in their own great hall, where John had snatched a bride from them. Their hurt pride, the treachery on the part of John and the Count of Angoulême, the connivance of others all boiled up. It was time to show that they were the lords of Lusignan.

Ralph rode home to Normandy and could not rid himself of the chafing memory; his trust in John vanished. The king had done wrong; there could be no more pledges and oaths. Ralph's domain was rich, he had resources – he would strike, but not alone. Arthur of Brittany would be a useful ally. His mother Constance was now married to a Poitevin, Guy of Thouars, and the Lusignans had long had alliances with this family.

Ralph wrote to Guy that he was keen to begin again, to assert Arthur's claims to the throne. Would Guy help?

Back in the Poitevin, Hugh considered his options. He would take his cause to the king, the French king who, after all, could call on John as a vassal, as the Duke of Aquitaine who had sworn fealty to Philippe. He could order John, but to do what? Hugh thought about Philippe and his likely moves against John: would he order him to pay some large sum of money, a punitive fine, take away a castle, call on the Pope? Whatever happened Hugh would not get Isabella back.

*

Aimery de Thouars arrived at Fontevraud where Eleanor received him, sitting in a high-backed chair, the fire lit to take the chill off the stone walls.

'You are making a good continued convalescent?' Aimery was solicitous and comforting.

Eleanor pulled her woollen shawl closer and regarded this man, the Poitevin baron who had, so far, not caused her family any injury. 'Welcome, well-beloved cousin. I believe you know the situation. The Lusignans are protesting about Isabella, indeed some could call it a rebellion – I fear they will go to Philippe. The heritage we have here, that I guard for John, will be torn asunder if we cannot make sure of obedience in those lands, in those castles that are prepared to do so much wrong to us, bring so much shame on us.'

Aimery listened. Here were difficulties: kinsmen were involved in Brittany and Anjou – was he strong and clever enough to thwart their plans? He was Eleanor's most powerful vassal, that they both knew. But his younger brother had married Constance of Brittany and now had Arthur as a stepson – Arthur, the nephew of Richard and John. Many believed he had a better claim to the English throne than a younger brother. And the younger brother, the treacherous John, had used Aimery badly before.

'I helped at the beginning,' he began cautiously, 'when John was scrambling for support. I was with those mercenaries who sacked Anjou and went on to take Le Mans.'

'And he rewarded you?'

'He did, oh yes, but then he scorned me – his gifts are given and then snatched away.'

In silence, they both considered John and his unstable behaviour.

Aimery's thoughts ran on: Eleanor was the Duchess of Aquitaine still, she had once been the Queen of France and of England, and her granddaughter Blanche was now married to Prince Louis who would be king. Eleanor's son, the last of her sons, this King John, he may well have abilities and power that would triumph. Which way to turn, whose side to take? Aimery twisted his hands together in front of the fire and made his choice.

In London letters arrived from France: wars and rumours of wars, and the dreams of pleasure were shaken awake.

> *I have been very ill but I want to tell you, my dear son, that I summoned Aimery de Thouars to visit me during my illness and he has promised to do everything he can to bring back those disobedient barons and counts who defy your authority. We need to hold, or indeed regain, lands and castles. I was much comforted by his presence.*

And not only a letter from his mother, but one from her secretary too, saying much the same. Guy assured John that Eleanor's concerns were not merely the worries of an old woman. And yet another letter from Aimery, also full of warnings and protesting his loyalty.

John sat looking down at the letters with a faint sneer. He could afford to wait a little before making a journey to France. Meanwhile he would deal with Ralph in Normandy, and so he dashed off a letter to his officials in Rouen: *Do Ralph all the harm you can manage, harry the man and make his life uncomfortable.*

And as for Hugh, well he would make sure that La Marche went at once to the Count of Angoulême. Oh, he had promised it last year but delayed the order for the gifting to a new owner. Perhaps he had felt that Hugh had had enough taken away from him, but Isabella's parents had been very helpful with her capture and delivery to him. So he penned another letter, this time to Poitiers to sort out the land deeds for La Marche.

A delighted Count of Angoulême wrote back at once: *My support for your campaign of pester and plunder and siege of the Lusignan castles is assured.*

And indeed, the castles were being more than besieged: they were being seized.

Isabella stood at the window of her chamber overlooking the Thames. She had seen the messengers arrive – Agnes had told her they were from France, bringing letters from Eleanor and others, all with news about the Lusignans. Did they care what had happened to her? Was it true that Hugh was going to marry her cousin Mathilde? It seemed likely that he would want that alliance between Angoulême and Lusignan made in some way. She longed for news of home and her parents had not written since before Christmas, when they had been so full of the reports of her coronation. She had written from the north when life had been cold and enclosed with no lively court life to boast about, only endless journeys on foul roads or living in gaunt castles where the wind pierced the stone and everyone huddled around smoky fires. She stamped her foot in impatience – was her life to be spent waiting to be told about events? She wanted to be part of them, marvelled at, not carried around the country like some pet dog.

'My sweeting, so cross and foolish! I have letters here that tell of Hugh and Ralph – their lives are very grim now you have left the Poitevin.'

John held the letters high above her head, teasing Isabella who whirled about trying to snatch them from him.

'Not so fast, my lady – we must take care of these, they tell of disloyalty and treachery. But now I have written to your father to make sure of La Marche, for did I not promise that to him?'

'You did, and you promised me Niort and Saintes, to add

117

to my own Angoulême. I will need the tithes from these lands to keep my own court.'

'Your own court indeed! Such pride, Isabella, and who will be at your court? Will you fill it with Poitevins and Angoumois? A wild court that would be.'

And he swept her out of the room into the king's chambers. His scribe was waiting for the letters to make sure they were tied up and safely stored. John almost threw the letters at him and turned to Isabella, who stood tall, graceful, mockingly submissive, her eyes bright and wary.

'Who can coo and who can hiss? No one like you, Isabella. I swear you have the blood of Melusine even if your family denies this, or did Melusine visit you in Lusignan, teach you before your time how to strut?'

'There is no secret, no heart of it. Let be, my lord.'

The scribe scuttled out, rolling the parchment and smoothing vellum as he went, nervous and anxious to leave this room where passions were running so high.

Letters continued, and messages were sent in a flurry of angry activity. Ralph and Hugh appealed to King Philippe.

Sire: you are the ultimate overlord for France; we are seeking justice. Driencourt Castle has been seized, La Marche given to the Count of Angoulême. Isabella was kidnapped by John, larceny of the highest order. He has attacked us, despoilt our name.

Philippe sat in his library in La Conciergerie, Le Palais de la Cité and turned the letter over. He wished it had not been written. It was impossible to ignore this appeal but he was not over-eager or indeed very willing to support the Lusignan brothers in their rebellion. He would need to tread carefully. His own affairs were precarious: a marriage that had been declared bigamous – indeed it *was* bigamous, however much he pretended it was not. An interdict from the Pope had been recently lifted, it was true, but he had to proceed gingerly at this precarious time. And hadn't he and John signed the Treaty of Le Goulet? A truce that need not be broken over these brothers, who were capable of changing sides so easily.

He considered the options. He wasn't ready to send any troops or armed men to help them – it didn't suit his purposes at the moment, and John had mustered a very impressive force last year. No, he thought – it was not an expedition to be taken lightly. So he sat tight – he'd heard that John was planning to cross the Channel and visit Normandy and Aquitaine, so Philippe would wait until then. Perhaps a visit to the Norman border, an invitation to Paris – that was a way forward, to cement the friendship between Capet and Angevin. The Lusignans would have to stop harassing the government at Poitou while John and Philippe agreed some amicable arrangement.

John liked Portsmouth; there was a good harbour on that inlet, and it was close to London. A good place to call for his knights and vassals to assemble for a campaign. It was the ideal location from which his fleet could set sail for France, where he would deal with that rebellion. Now the town was busy with the weekly market and the local court was in session. All well and good, and John decided to issue another charter, making sure that the rights and privileges that had been awarded to the town were reaffirmed. He would make sure it was paid for, though: 10 marks and a horse, a palfrey.

And he could wait in comfort in the King's House, that fortified manor house built by brother Richard. Wait for the wind and the tide to be right for a crossing. Send for money, if needed, from the treasury at Winchester, or send money there if he collected taxes. Indeed, the more he thought about it the more he thought that this would make a useful permanent naval base. Plans could be drawn, stone ordered from Caen, building work organised.

And now the barons and the knights were trooping in, eager for some action, their baggage carts nicely full. There were protests as their money was taken, all those marks brought here for their own expenses but now in John's treasury. Grumbling, they went home.

'That was a shoddy trick, he'll use the money to pay mercenaries and we had no say in any of it.'

'Shifty *and* shoddy – I do not take kindly to being treated in such a manner.'

John didn't care – it had been swift and easy this way, and he was tired of the resistance the barons brought to any decision-making.

Isabella listened to the plans for the new naval town, the plans for the sea journey, but in her mind she was already in France. John had not promised that they would visit Angoulême, but she hoped they would. Meanwhile she could think about where they were to stay first: the Château Gaillard, that great Angevin castle built by Richard, and one of the strongest defences in the Norman boundaries against Philippe.

'And one of the costliest – thousands, my brother spent on that place, double the money he spent on any castle in England,' John mused. 'How he loved it – he made all the plans himself, spent much time there, supervising and helping. The quarries worked overtime, masons, carpenters, smiths. Workmen by the hundred, and finished so quickly, less than two years.'

Isabella dreamt on, imagining herself sweeping through the corridors, taking leisurely walks in the gardens, until he suddenly stopped and caught her under the chin, staring fiercely into her face.

'There could be a curse on it, Isabella. Have you heard

how labourers working on the castle were drenched in a rain of blood? Many advisers thought the rain was an evil omen – so would I, wouldn't you? But Richard was not moved by this, he would not slacken the pace of the work. He would have cursed an angel if one had descended from Heaven and urged him to abandon the building. He called the château his daughter and boasted that he could hold it even if the walls were made of butter.'

And then he was gone, calling for news about the wind, the weather and tides.

By the end of May they could sail for Barfleur, not together as when they had crossed to England for the coronation, but on separate ships. The weather turned rough; some said because of the total eclipse of the moon that lasted for three hours – a full moon that was supposed to bring a big tide to help them on their way. Isabella's ship sailed fast and free, cutting through great waves to Barfleur, but the stress of the storm sent the captain of the royal ship running to the Isle of Wight for shelter.

John arrived, angry with the weather and the captain's decision. He stormed into the manor house where Isabella waited. Agnes was sitting nearby, now recovered from her seasickness but still wan and peaky.

'She looks like a newly hatched bird, all damp and spindly,' growled John. 'Not much help for you – send her home.'

Isabella ignored him and signalled for Agnes to leave the room before he acted on this worrying idea.

'We ride to Gaillard tomorrow. Time to establish ourselves there.'

Isabella handed him a letter. 'This was waiting for you. I have not opened it, but it came from Philippe.'

John glanced at her. 'No, you would be well advised to

keep your hands and prying eyes away from any letters of mine.'

Isabella almost flew at him as he took the letter, but remembering his temper and his threat about Agnes, held back. She put her hands behind her back and waited for the contents to be read to her.

'Well, well. The French king, Monsieur Philippe, is to meet us at the boundary with France. Our Norman lands are still strong...good. We can resolve Lusignan matters with ease, I think.'

XI

Paris was exploding with buildings, trades, new churches, new palaces and new walls. Philippe commanded his small but growing city from the Île de la Cité in the Seine – solid rock foundations here, and mudflats everywhere else. He had met John and Isabella at the frontiers of Normandy, and now led them into the Palace de la Cité.

'I have ordered everything for you to be of great comfort. Indeed, I am moving out to the Louvre – the Palace of the Wolves, some call it. But my wolf-hunting dogs have their own kennels.'

John laughed. He and Philippe had been united against Richard once before, and he remembered hunting with this ally when he was trying to wrest the English crown for himself. It was strange to think that Philippe was only two years older than him. He had been king since he was fifteen; taking on responsibilities, and it seemed to John that he had become more serious and self-disciplined, but always with a nervous edge. And without doubt, clever and wily. But now John was a king on equal terms with Philippe, except for that small matter of the Treaty of Goulet and his fealty to him as the Duke of Aquitaine.

'And your city has its own walls – God's teeth, they are

formidable. So many towers to look across to Normandy.'

'We have indeed been troubled from that quarter in the past.'

Philippe had tried hard to out-fool that crafty man, Henry II, and had been more than willing to set brother against brother, sons against father; to split the Angevins. And John – what kind of a king was he going to be? He still owed Philippe money from the signing the previous year in Goulet.

Isabella was at a window, looking back to where they had ridden in through a fortified gateway. 'We passed a great hill as we approached, so high on the plain. There was a village and an abbey, there were fields of wheat and vines – I think the harvest was being gathered in. Were there working mills too? It reminded me of the hills near Angoulême.'

Philippe considered Isabella: his second cousin, wife of John, daughter of his cousin Alice. An important heiress and a considered beauty; the Lusignans thought her worth a fight or two. He would have to use some diplomacy with John and Hugh; he did not want a war to arouse the Pope. He had only just managed to get the interdict on France lifted. Mass could be celebrated again and all the important religious rituals observed. The country had heaved a sigh of relief. Philippe sighed too, but his detested lawful wife was supposed to be with him again, and Agnes of Méran, that wonderful woman whom he loved above all others, had taken herself away to a closed convent. This was not as he wanted it at all, but France must come first, always. And the two palaces were full of young people: his children by Agnes, and Prince Louis, his son from his first marriage. Thirteen now, the same age as his young wife Blanche, who was, he reminded himself, John's niece. They were all waiting to meet these important guests. It would be better to turn the conversation to the glories of Paris than think about the trouble that John could cause.

'It was an easy journey for you from Rouen? The roads are fast and the countryside is flat, good riding I think. And here in Paris there are now streets paved with stone. The stench from the waste from the houses mixed in with the mud made our city unbearable. I am more than determined to make this city a great capital of France.'

'And the hill we saw, that is not yet part of Paris?'

'No, but there are stories about it that connect it to our churches. It is called the Mount of Martyrs. St Dennis was martyred on that hill – pagan tribes took him there to put him to death at the temple of Mercury on top of the hill. But, being lazy and tired, they beheaded him halfway up, and he picked up his head and continued to the fountain where he washed the blood away and then carried on for a few more leagues before collapsing and being buried.' Philippe gestured to the door that led to the interior rooms. 'My son, who waits to meet you, he will tell you all the stories about the holy men and women of the church – he is a good scholar and studies well. He could also show you the Notre Dame, our new cathedral.'

Isabella continued to look back to the road they had travelled. Paris was exciting and different, and yet she felt at home here – this was her country, far more than England was, although the Poitevin was where she belonged. She shook her head. Do not think about home; think about something closer. She wondered what Blanche would be like; they were about the same age. She knew she had been fetched from Spain by her grandmother, Eleanor. And that John and Philippe had arranged the marriage between Louis and Blanche, except it had been the older sister of Blanche who had been suggested first, but then Eleanor had chosen Blanche as a better queen for France. So everyone changed their minds about who would be the bride, the queen, the consort – it was not just John who upset marriage plans. What made Blanche better than her sister? And what of Louis? A young prince and husband for Blanche; the couple were both the same age. Not married in Paris, though, because the Pope had put that interdict on France, accusing Philippe of bigamy, so no church bells, no Mass, and the marriage had taken place in John's Norman lands, away from here.

And now those two were talking politics and boundaries. She heard Hugh de Lusignan's name mentioned and was downcast – she had not thought of him for months. He had been generous and kind, making sure she was looked after and taught how to behave. Lusignan seemed a very long time ago, that time of learning and preparation for becoming the countess. Queen consort now, and no more lessons in etiquette and management of a household, no more arithmetic. Feasts and journeys, castles and coronations, a bewildering mix of heady indulgence and boredom.

'You are Isabella, the new Queen of England, married to my uncle.'

Blanche, demure, quiet but very sure of herself, stood with Prince Louis in the long gallery by the river. His nervous eyes darted from Isabella's feet to her hair, anxious not to be seen examining her too closely.

Isabella was pleased that she was wearing her fine blue silk with its heavy silver embroidery; she needed to be seen as important in front of this couple. Blanche had a forceful way with her, as young as she was. She is very like her grandmother, thought Isabella, but I am taller than her. And she walked forward slowly and deliberately past the pair of them to look at the river.

'A fine river here in Paris. It surrounds this island?'

'At night chains are lowered so no boats can creep up onto the shore, the defences are admirable. It is a fortress against our enemies – we keep here a mighty arsenal protected by that great tower.' Louis was determined to show this Isabella that he knew about his city and all its glories. 'And we have a fine new cathedral. They are beginning to build and decorate the façade now. It is the cathedral for all the kings of Europe. And there is to be a university for scholars to study theology, across the river where we have new monasteries too.'

Isabella yawned – this was boasting prattle, she thought, and this young prince was boring.

Blanche saw the yawn. 'You are tired? Would you like to take some air? We can walk a little around the square before the welcome feast in your honour.'

All three made their way down the long gallery, Isabella walking in front of them, swishing her skirts in a proud and irritating manner, lifting the hem of her gown to show off new soft leather boots embroidered around the ankle.

'A present from my husband, the king,' she said, knowing that Louis and Blanche were watching as they walked after her with quiet decorum.

Philippe was intent on making this state visit a triumph, and had called for the pale wine from Reims to be served.

'My Capet ancestor drank this first at his coronation. We serve it to honoured guests.'

He wanted John to listen to him and he hoped the wine would make him receptive to advice. They would speak face to face, with no one else within hearing, so to this end he met John in the antechamber and together, beakers in hand, they walked about the room.

'I will not press you on this appeal from the Lusignans to me. It is an embarrassment but you must be seen to carry out your duty and give them the chance to bring their griev-ances to court, and I will ask them to stop besieging Poitou. I can mediate and we can smooth it all over. Oil on troubled waters – do you not think that is the best way to behave? We must not forget that Isabella was a prize indeed, and you have her.'

Arms around shoulders, some mutual backslapping – a good compromise, thought Philippe as they rejoined the long tables in the hall. He looked at his young son and his assured young wife, falling in love with each other, he hoped; he wished for grandsons and if they loved each other it would help. Too young presently, but it would come.

A disturbance as John sat down heavily next to Isabella and twisted her hair in his hands as he turned her to him, kissing her hard. Blanche and Louis stared and then looked away.

An amicable parting at the end of the week, and the two rivals agreed they had made a sensible solution to the Lusignan problem. Glowing with good-natured appreciation of the visit to Paris, John was happily ready to leave. He felt masterful and dominant again and thought Philippe's compromise showed a weakness. Surely he was hiding something.

Louis and Blanche made polite noises as they made their farewells to Isabella, who looked mockingly at them both. She knew so much more than they did, that pair of holy mice.

'We ride to Chinon now, Berengaria is lodging there. I may be able to settle her widow's dowry at last.'

Chinon was a good place to be in the summer months, the castle a favourite of all the Angevin kings, overlooking the River Vienne as it flowed towards the Loire through fertile fields. Aquitaine was peaceful. Isabella's father was tamping down the discontent, ably helped by Aimery de Thouars. The mercenaries had stayed in France with John, guaranteeing fair words from Philippe, it seemed. Eleanor's worried letters to John, setting out her fears, were to be ignored. Now was the best time for long, lazy mornings with Isabella, hunting in the afternoon, dice and wine in the evenings.

In early August as all turned to the harvest, news arrived from Paris.

'Philippe's mistress – his wife, except the Pope would not allow it – has died.'

'Agnes of Méran has died? That will help set things straight for him.'

And indeed Philippe was already appealing to Innocent to legitimise his children by Agnes. His royal position had become stronger, free of matrimonial confusion. He had no intention of living with that Danish wife; she could continue to shift about the various castles and towns, as long as she kept out of his way. He still shuddered when he thought of their wedding night: she was full of sorcery, of that he was convinced, and he would not spend any time with her. He would make sure that Philippe and Marie were safe as his heirs, along with Louis. Then when that was accomplished, he could turn his mind to John's dispute with the Lusignans. It was very possible that this could be a lever to help him achieve his dream: to break up the power of the English in France.

More news of another death. Early September brought riders from Brittany, from Nantes. 'Arthur's mother Constance has died, the twin daughters live.'

Isabella felt ill as John told the story of the complicated birth, a forty-year-old mother weakened, they thought, by leprosy, and then to have two babies to thrust into the world. She shuddered – when would she have to go through this ordeal? Not yet, not this year.

'We were reconciled before the end.' John smirked a little. 'At last she stopped being so aggressive towards my being king instead of Arthur. That widow of my brother was always troublesome, but now she is gone. And I will make sure her bequests are made and her memory honoured.'

*

'Your king is very high-spirited these days.' Agnes was mending a chemise with tiny stitches. Isabella had wound the thread for her and was playing with the sewing basket, sorting the pins into a silver pin case.

'He is pleased to have been in Paris and agreed with the French king to allow the Lusignans a trial at court.'

But Isabella felt unsure that there would be a trial as expected. John was high-handed, crowing whenever their name was mentioned as he drew up the documents. He was so over-confident, so cocksure.

'That once-upon-a-time future husband of yours – what grand gestures! Seeking to make a case for redress at my court in front of all the barons. I have other plans for them. My own way will cramp and quell them.'

Isabella squirmed in his arms. She was beginning to realise that all his plans seemed to be about punishing and kicking people. And then everything happened very quickly. The Lusignans were charged with treason.

Prove your innocence, Hugh! Ralph! In the ancient way, the honourable way that was used by past kings for traitors, fight for your innocence, fight my champions.

Among John's mercenaries were several such men, skilled and powerful, well paid and ready to fight a judicial duel and vanquish the two brothers.

'This is a provocation that cannot be borne – he is intent on humiliation again. He challenges all Lusignans and claims we have committed treason against him and against Richard.'

Ralph seethed as he and Hugh read through the document: treason, innocence and traitors. It was not to be accepted, this abasement of all their pride. 'He expects us to fight professional duellists, to lose our lives as well as everything else. We are not answerable to him, but he denies us justice.'

Hugh appealed to Philippe.

You are the supreme overlord in this matter; this Duke of Aquitaine goes too far. Trial by combat is a mockery. Ralph Lusignan, my brother the Count of Eu, has renounced his oaths to John, and we are set on a fair trial. We will answer to no one save our peers.

A remonstration to John, no longer our dearly beloved. A pressing message from Philippe: *You must promise that a fair trial will be held. Do not prevaricate again.*
A shifty reply from John.

I have set the date more than once, but they refused it, saying that without a safe conduct they would not attend. So my offer was made, but so was a refusal.

Philippe heard these slippery excuses and made decisions; John was flouting his authority, pushing at his own command of feudal provincial lords, and threatening his prestige. A trial would happen and he ordered John to surrender castles as sureties for his appearance at Philippe's court.

'He wants Falaise and Gaillard! I think not, by God's truth.'

And so letters were sent summoning Hubert Walter. These brought the Archbishop of Canterbury to Paris just before Christmas, and he arrived with a set of elaborate excuses; a rigmarole of words designed to stall. And so another delay as the New Year came in, and then Easter brought an irritated summons from Philippe.

My patience and diplomacy are exhausted and now you will come to Paris, before my barons, and answer for this injustice.

Another tricky answer.

I do believe by ancient agreement that as Duke of Normandy I need only appear before such a court when it meets on our boundaries.

Philippe wrote in exasperation.

I am summoning you as Duke of Aquitaine, Count of Anjou and Count of Poitou. As such you are my vassal and will appear at my court. As Gaillard and Falaise are not to be made hostage for you, then I am demanding two others that I will have this time: Boutavant and Tillères.

John growled at Isabella as they walked the grounds in Chinon.

'I have surrendered those two castles in Brittany – by the bowels of Christ, he will not have any piece of Normandy. I am being cornered over these Lusignans – why didn't they agree to fight my champions? It would all be over now.'

'Perhaps it was considered an intolerable insult.'

'An insult, you think! Who are you to stand by them, to defend that man? You are married to me, and remember I am your king and your husband. Watch your words carefully.'

Isabella stood still and faced him. She was trembling a little; this was not how she was used to being spoken to by anyone, and this husband who had taken her into his bed and used her had also woken something in her.

'I must speak as someone who knows well the Lusignan lords, and they are not a humble family.'

'You think you know them? Well, I will grant you that you have spent longer under their roof than I have, but all those Poitevins are treacherous, and in that I include your Angoulême father.'

Isabella's hand was at his face, but he caught it and twisted her arm behind her back.

'Enough, my spiteful little queen, we might like this quarrel too much. Your spirit is hot which does not displease me, but not when we are talking about Hugh le Brun. Go, find Agnes and Berengaria and pray for our victory over all who are against us. And as for Philippe, I will make another promise to him and he can have a border castle or two if that will appease him for now. Sureties can be given if necessary.'

Isabella sat in her chamber, tired and wary of promises. Where was her income for her own court? And here they were in Chinon with Berengaria; she had been queen to Richard and John was only now arranging a proper widow's dowry for her. And his mother, Eleanor, another Queen of England, living close by. And in Marlborough, Avisa of Gloucester, still supported by John. It seemed there were many queens of England, and Isabella was the least considered.

'He will not keep his promise, Agnes – he will not surrender those castles. I know how he bullies everyone whom he thinks weaker than him, and how he plays games with those on his level, always trying to tweak at them. The Lusignans will fight and then my father will fight them.'

She crumpled onto the bed, and Agnes sat and stroked her back, murmuring soothing words but no real comfort.

Philippe considered the situation. He had, for a while, accepted John, a powerful neighbour, an old ally, close to Paris. Normandy was just across the Seine, the Vexin plateau divided between them. But now John was behaving so badly over this local wrangle that it was time to take advantage of an incompetent and bad tempered King. He spoke to his court, a decision made.

'He has not appeared, nor made surrender of the castles. He has not obeyed the citation, so my lords, what we now proclaim is this: that John, Duke of Aquitaine is a contumacious vassal. The assembled court of the King of France will adjudge the King of England to be deprived of all his land which he and his forefathers had hitherto held of the King of France. We declare his fiefdoms of Aquitaine, Poitou and Anjou forfeit. We here pronounce that all feudal ties between ourselves and John are severed. Our forces will attack the boundaries with Normandy.'

XII

Chinon and Mirebeau, 1202

Gournay, just east of Rouen, was small and quiet, a rural backwater known only for its little mottled chickens, which laid well and tasted good. And here in a square next to church stood Arthur, fifteen, slight, fair-haired, bare-headed, but Prince of Brittany, about to be knighted by Philippe, about to swear allegiance, to pay homage to the French king. He knelt and said the words which tied him to Philippe; it was more than a personal allegiance – there was great significance. The homage was for the Angevin lands and territories.

Philippe handed his four-year-old daughter towards Arthur. A good betrothal, he thought, better than the one he had arranged when Marie was two, to the Prince of Scotland. He had broken that one to arrange this. Now to make sure the two hundred French knights were ready for Arthur to lead.

'You must ride south and take possession of your inheritance. The Poitevins are poised to help you – the Lusignan brothers, Raymond of Toulouse, the Count of Limoges have all joined together, and members of the Thouars family whom you know well. Godspeed, be loyal, be bold, cross the Loire and victory is yours.'

The noise of the horses, the clamour of the knights as they shouted one to the other, skilled and trained horsemen.

All individuals that Arthur now had to make work together, as they rode towards Tours, planning the route south to the coveted and vulnerable Poitevin lands that were Angevin territory.

It was the worst outcome that Eleanor could have feared. Not only had John stirred and poked and riled the Lusignans, who had found plenty of rebellious Poitevin lords to come to their side, but he had caused so many problems of duty and loyalty for Philippe that the French king had now taken Arthur entirely to his court and sent him off to fight for the Angevin lands that belonged to the English crown. She struggled out of her chair and called her secretary to her.

'We must ride to Poitiers and make sure it is defended against these traitors and rebels. It is my capital, the heart-land of the Angevin territory. If I am there Arthur cannot take it. I will not allow John to be dispossessed of all that is ours.'

A small escort guard was hastily formed, but the men knew that progress would be slow: Eleanor could not ride all the way to Poitiers these days, but must be carried in a litter for part of the journey.

The late July heat had made the roads dusty and rutted, and as it grew dark they were within twenty miles of Poitiers. Too far to continue that night.

'If necessary we could use the old castle at Mirebeau for lodgings. It was once a good stronghold for the Anjou family, but is crumbling now.'

They made for the inner hall and settled in with as much comfort as possible.

John paced with anger through the rooms at Le Mans. Philippe was biting away at his defences in the east of Normandy, trying to break through the protective shield of good, stout, stone castles. The Normans knew how to build a wall against marauders and John was not ready to take the fight out and away from them yet.

'Where are the recruiting men? I sent them to find more mercenaries – we need more men.'

It was all in hand, Peter des Roches explained: the money was enough and the extra forces would arrive. Indeed, they were eager for work. Their usual allies, the Rhineland princes, had departed on a crusade, and the best mercenaries came from those countries.

'If the princes were not so intent on saving their souls in a crusade they could be taking Philippe by surprise now, charging in from the rear.'

John swore and paced and bit his knuckles. His thoughts were dark and bitter – bitter towards the nephew who had twisted this way and that, and now declared himself the rightful heir and dared to fight against his king. Arthur, Geoffrey's boy, born after his father died. Well, that brother was the worst of them all. A good friend of Philippe of France, and they had often plotted together against Henry. Indeed, Geoffrey had spent so much time at Philippe's court that he was made a seneschal.

'They said I was a traitor against my father, but Geoffrey rebelled the most, and his words, his cunning, lying words, were so honeyed, so eloquent that he could dissolve all alliances and confuse every king who listened. And now his son turns against me.'

Prince Arthur was enjoying the bold sally down the valley of the Loire, banners streaming as more knights joined with his. His two hundred had become two hundred and fifty, and here was another Lusignan, another brother of Hugh, someone who had fought in the Holy Land and would be a warrior worth having on his side. And this one had good reason to hate John, who had taken his castle in Moncontour. The Lusignans had made sure they were banded together in this rebellion.

Tours was a good place to stop before considering the next move. The crossroads of their territories, rich and with its own currency. The castle built by Arthur's grandfather could accommodate them all. He swaggered a little as he dismounted and gave orders. It was a fine evening and there would be a plentiful meal after the long ride.

'There is interesting news.' A local lord approached Arthur as he speared chunks of meat and slurped at some wine. 'Your grandmother is not far from here. Lodged in Mirebeau which is a poor castle, and easy to besiege.'

Arthur remembered how she had made him swear to be loyal, to keep within the fold, to deny his inheritance. He would not follow her advice now that he had her at his mercy. But it would be wise to proceed with caution; possibly more men would be needed for such a daring plan to succeed. Could he raise a few hundred more in time? The Lusignans thought not – their combined force would have to be sufficient.

'We could take her and make her a hostage. It would be a most useful ploy.'

'She could be bartered for Isabella, an old queen for a new queen.'

The Poitevins and all the knights thumped the table in agreement.

'If we capture her, John's position here would collapse. Without her the southwest would turn away from him, we could ask for anything and get it.'

But Eleanor knew her value as a hostage only too well, and she gave instructions to her men-at-arms to prepare for defence.

'We will not give in to that grandson who dares to threaten. But we are not provisioned for a siege, and our defences are somewhat weak. So make haste to send out two messengers while we are still able. One to ride to John – he must bring me aid as soon as possible. And another must ride to Chinon and alert William des Roches, the Seneschal of Anjou. Summon him, for he is a strong leader of men and we need him at this hour.'

Agnes was worrying about the fighting. Oliver was with John at Le Mans, and they had not seen each other for some days before he left, not been able to say goodbye. She thought Isabella was sulking, bored without the admiring circle which had been around her all summer. Such a lazy, luxurious summer. And Isabella had become haughtier than ever, disdainful of anyone who suggested she should be a little more careful.

'I am now the Countess of Angoulême,' she reminded Agnes, 'since my father died. He did not live to fight Hugh Lusignan after all. I have come into my inheritance, in my own right. I should be considered most important in these territories, a Queen of England and someone who has dowry lands so close by.'

'And will John give you control of what is yours, my lady? I hear he has plans to appoint a governor to administer all. And what of your mother? Is she not ruling Angoulême?'

'She may be for now as she has her widow's dower rights. I am to be in charge of what is mine – my parents promised me that county and it is what I want too.'

But these fine words were just that: fine words. Isabella begged to go back to her home to see her mother and to make her claims public, to show herself to the people, her people. She was laughed to scorn and taken to bed to be shown who was the master and ruler.

And then John had given her jewels to wear, something that she seemed to enjoy more than the fine clothes. It was unlike John to give anything without good reason, and Agnes suspected that the lust he felt for Isabella was lulling him at last into generosity, or that he felt some guilt over his refusal to see her hunger for what was her own.

Isabella trailed into the room, her face petulant. Agnes eyed her keenly: was this spoilt fourteen-year-old girl pining for her husband? She no longer looked like the frightened virgin who had been snatched away from the Lusignans, from Hugh who had waited for her. She looked less innocent, more knowing, and had a certain sensual sway to her walk, even when she was sullen.

'Look, Agnes.' And she put out her arms to show a new bracelet, a thick band of gold, studded with pearls and garnets. 'It belonged to his grandmother, Matilda – she was the Holy Roman Empress, Empress of Germany, and all her jewellery is here in Chinon. But he said that I was the greatest treasure and worth more than all the gold from Germany. He needed to make me sweet again after angry words.'

Agnes bit her lip and continued with her embroidery. 'Come, why not join me and we can stitch some roses onto this sleeve?'

Reluctantly Isabella threaded a needle and picked at the linen. It was many months since she had been quiet and working at something with Agnes. A small part of her resisted but it was peaceful to be so employed.

'Everyone has gone from Chinon except Berengaria, who is forever at her prayers. She appears to be planning how to use her dower lands nearby, if she is ever given them.'

'That is a sour thought, Isabella.'

'John makes these promises and hands out lands and towns with ease, but there seems to be nothing in the end to hold onto, to own. That is why this gift.' She stopped sewing to admire the bracelet again. 'And that is why I am so full of joy to have this.'

'To have what?' Berengaria paused in the doorway and felt a deep melancholy as she looked at Isabella. It was wrong that one so young should be here in this position. 'A bracelet?

It is very fine, if you want earthly things. But even gold can be corrupted.'

She came in and sat on a stool near Isabella.

'I had rich jewellery from Richard when we married, but it all went to help buy his ransom. And I have very little of anything now, except the dower lands I am promised by John at Le Mans and Anjou. I am not as fortunate as my sister.'

'And you have lands in England too?' Isabella was interested to know about these, because at times John promised her more domains for her royal revenue, her queen's gold.

'Yes, and I wish that John would compensate me for them. I would have more here in France. I have never been to England, I have no desire to be there. I wish to remain here, near Chinon. My one purpose now is to build a religious foundation, near here where I feel at peace.'

'How pious you are!'

'It is a way of life that appeals to me, has long appealed to me. My early life was all chaos and confusion. The betrothal to Richard and then that long and difficult journey to join him. Oh, it was dreadful! First to Sicily with Eleanor – that is where I met his sister. Joan was a good friend to me. Then as we travelled on towards the Holy Land, a storm drove the ship aground in Cyprus. And we were threatened there, refused shelter, insulted and denied water by the ruler.'

Agnes exclaimed, 'Poor ladies, to be so scorned.'

Berengaria plucked at her girdle, twisting the silk around her fingers, and then she smiled up at them. A joyful memory. 'But Richard came to rescue us and conquer the island, and we were married there. And after that the crusade and the journey back to France. It was a time of great fear and danger… Richard's capture and imprisonment. His ransom…and I am ever mindful of Châlus, his death. My time has been all distress. As you can see and witness, what I wish most in this world is to settle into a life full of prayer.'

Isabella broke in. 'And there were Lusignans in Cyprus with Richard? Some story I heard?'

'Indeed, Guy Lusignan arrived from Jerusalem, always ambitious, always looking for power or a title. He helped defeat the wicked man who ruled there and claimed to be emperor. No emperor at all, just an upstart governor. Guy went with Richard to finish the crusade and Richard sold Cyprus to the Knights Templar – oh, so severe and ruthless as rulers. Massacres ensued, misery ran with the blood in the streets, and the people begged Richard to take back the island, and he did. And then Guy was pushed out of Jerusalem after his wife died – he was not wanted as king, for sure – and Richard offered him Cyprus, and so there he was, a childless king. His brother has now inherited the island.'

'So there are Lusignans there, kings indeed.'

'But you should know, Isabella, that Guy and his brother were men who did great wrong, they have done mischief in the Poitou. They killed a man who was returning from a pilgrimage, they ambushed and killed the Earl of Salisbury and Richard, as their overlord, as Duke of Aquitaine, banished them. The world is full of such relentless wrongdoing. I would be apart from it.'

Berengaria finished her story flushed, for once not looking so sad. Then she stood, smoothing down her skirts, bade them a good night's rest and left, as downcast as always.

'There is a lady glad to be out of the storm of courts and kings.'

'Do you think I am in the middle of a storm, Agnes?'

'Yes I do, it is not of your making but a tempest is breaking now and you are in the centre.'

Agnes finished the petal she was embroidering and they held hands and sat quietly as the room darkened in the late July dusk.

*

Arthur had reached Mirebeau. The outer walls were easily breached and he ordered all but one of the gates to be barricaded, earthed up, so no one could enter or leave without being seen by his soldiers. His supplies would come through this way too, but nothing must reach the castle where his grandmother had locked herself inside the keep. She was willing to talk to him, but that was all.

'*Grand-mère*, leave now with all your possessions and you are free to go wherever you wish, in peace.'

'I will not be ordered to leave one of my own castles by a prince who is not courteous. I am amazed that you, my grandson and the Poitevins, who are my liegemen, should think to besiege a castle that has Eleanor, Duchess of Aquitaine within.'

'Grandmother, I am assured by the King of France that you can have your freedom if you allow him a conclusion and settlement of your domains.'

'That is a statement of greed and wickedness, most greedy and most wicked. Spoken by a king to whom I swore fealty for these lands, which are mine by right of birth and inheritance. There are other castles to attack if you wish to learn how to make warfare – varlet, scallywag that you are.'

The courier's horse could be seen on the road, first a dusty blur and then the man was sliding from the saddle, holding the note that Eleanor had written and sealed with her ring.

John's reaction was swift and decisive. 'A detachment at once, make ready. It will be a forced march to Mirebeau, and none shall let up, day and night. Over eighty miles to cover and by God's will we will reach there to rescue my mother, the Queen Eleanor, from Arthur and the Lusignans.'

He swept along the road, his Angevin blood and temper firing his determination and resolution. This was not to be tolerated, an attack on his mother.

William des Roches caught up with him just outside

Chinon. 'I know that castle, I can lead the attack for you. We will be capable and successful, of that I can assure you. But you must assure me that you will hand me Arthur and the rebels to deal with if we capture them. Be guided by me in this.'

'I give you my word – you can take Arthur your prisoner.'

The exchange was made and William des Roches and his men galloped alongside and then ahead of John.

It was dawn on the first day of August when they reached Mirebeau. William and his troops burst through the one gate into the outer courtyard; a heavy assault, unexpected, on men scrambling to dress and arm themselves. Some rushed to get into the safety of the castle, but were so furiously pursued that this offered no shelter. The besiegers were taken, with nearly everyone killed or taken prisoner. And as Arthur was seized, John rode into the town. He helped his mother out of the keep and began arrangements for her to be escorted to safety.

'I will return to Fontevraud where life is peaceful. I long now for peace above all other states. The world is too full of strife and in Fontevraud I can be cloistered. But I must ask of you, indeed plead with you most forcefully: do not harm Arthur. He is of royal blood and an Angevin. You are his uncle – imprison him if you must. He has besieged his grandmother but I would not have him hurt for that.'

'Not only has he besieged you but been treasonable to me, he broke his oath and indeed he has made plain his plan to invade and conquer the Poitou. For this alone I would have him executed.'

Eleanor put her hand on his arm. 'You have been victorious here today – no one of importance has escaped. You have the strongest of positions with your worst enemies captured, the Lusignans and many French knights can be ransomed or used as valuable hostages. Let Arthur be.'

John bowed his head but did not answer, and Eleanor kissed his hand and left for the journey back to the abbey.

It was time to tell others about the brilliance of this battle, and John let no time slip by before he wrote to the English barons and William Marshall, exultant.

Know that by the Grace of God we are safe and well and God's mercy has worked wonderfully with us, for on Tuesday we heard that the lady our mother was closely besieged at Mirebeau, and we hurried there as fast as we could. And there we captured our nephew Arthur and Geoffrey de Lusignan, Hugh le Brun, Raymond de Thouars and all our other Poitevin enemies – not one escaped. Therefore God be praised for our happy success.

William Marshall, with the troops in Normandy, read the letter to them, to cheers and cries of triumph.

'Most heartening news, an excellent achievement.'

Then Marshall sent a taunting message across the lines to Ralph Lusignan: *The unhappy fate of your brothers. It seems we have them by the legs now.*

A very satisfied William Marshall was more than pleased to see the Lusignans curbed. He had seen his unarmed uncle murdered by them, had himself been captured by them, badly wounded and their prisoner for months until Eleanor had ransomed him. Yes, it was good to see the Lusignans humbled.

Philippe was badly shaken. Attacking castles on the Norman borders was forgotten and he hurried south to see what he could retrieve from the disaster, but it was too late.

John has the upper hand, he reported to Ralph Lusignan. I am at a loss to explain his fighting ability in the field. He has never been a warrior like his brothers, and now this! It is a grave misfortune, with much upset for me. We will order the troops we have to wreak vengeance on Tours, set fire to the place and plunder what we can.

And Philippe did that and returned to Paris to think hard about his next move.

On the road to the Loire the ox carts trundled, and they were full of the defeated and captured standing chained together. No heed was taken of who was manacled to whom – all ranks were bundled together, an ignominious spectacle. People came from their houses to see this parade of trophies, John's triumph.

'I will take my time, so all can see the fruits of that victory. Let this be a warning to those who defy me, turn traitor against their overlord. And we will ride past Chinon so that Isabella can see her Hugh le Brun. I have thoughts that he can be kept in France, in the tower in Caen. I will clear it of all other prisoners and he will be locked into the keep. Others will go to England, to Corfe Castle.'

William des Roches grinned. 'It was a glorious sight when we swept in to rout them. There they were, standing like babies, eating their breakfast – we caught Arthur, Prince of Brittany and Hugh Le Brun, that proud Lusignan, eating a breakfast of roasted pigeon. Well, they are a couple of squabs in a pot now!'

'And the rebellion has no leader with all captured, and all their vassals under my command and all their castles in my hands.'

John swung off his horse; he was supreme, confident, flushed with success. He joined William des Roches who stood by the Chinon gatehouse. And he made sure that Isabella was standing there too as the carts passed by.

'See, my lady – see what it means to be married to the king who vanquishes enemies. Look at that man whom you might have married – a sorry sight.'

Isabella raised her eyes to find Hugh le Brun standing shackled near the front of the cart. She quickly looked away

146

and turned to one side. John was treating his prisoners appallingly – this was not chivalrous, and this was not the code for knights and lords.

'Where is Arthur?' William des Roches was impatient; the deal had been made and he wanted Arthur as agreed. He had wanted the Poitevin lords too, but Arthur was the key piece.

John smirked; he did not care for this ambitious man. He may have the first voice in his council, he may have given him Anjou as a gift for switching to his side when he was securing his inheritance, but did he need him now? No.

'Arthur is in Falaise, in the dungeon, away from anyone's reach.'

'Are you forgetting the agreement we made on the road to Mirebeau? I was to be given Arthur, to say what would happen to him. You have gone back on your word, and not for the first time. The counties I control for you along the Loire are in safe hands with me, and this is how you reward me? And I can tell you that Aimery de Thouars, a friend to your mother, loyal to her, is full of horror to see his kinsmen in chains, in the carts, being treated like common thieves and murderers.'

William stared hard and angry at John, who had taken Isabella's shoulder and pulled her to his side, fondling her with increasing urgency. Power and lust were good bedfellows. Disgusted, des Roches pushed his way through the gawping crowd and found Aimery de Thouars outside.

'It is over,' he said curtly. 'We are not supporting that despicable lecher of a man anymore. Our allegiance will be to Philippe from now on. Others will follow us – see how he can hold onto Aquitaine when we have deserted his cause.'

XIII

The autumn came, and with it the fruit picked and the crops gathered in. For Aimery de Thouars and William des Roches the town of Angers and the surrounding countryside was their harvest. Other lords joined them, all demanding that John release Arthur from the dungeon in Falaise.

'Their allegiance shifts with the tides and the winds. Philippe has declared that I am not the King of England – well, that King of France can try to deny me my crown. And those two over-mighty lords, giving me orders! They think they can be with Philippe and with Arthur. They think to see Arthur in my place. They see a mighty omen in his name. A fabulous Arthur, an Arthur of the legends.'

Furious messages were sent to Falaise, messages that spoke of blinding and castrating Arthur, making him no threat in any way.

De Burgh, in charge of Arthur's captivity, defied the three men sent to take out his eyes and slice off his genitals. 'Leave here, leave here – the prince will not be touched by the likes of you, and King John will repent of such an action when his temper has shrunk. It would be a detestable deed, and one guaranteed to make the Bretons rise against him. Go back to Chinon and say that this ugly deed was not to be done.'

The rage died down and no one acted on the angry, barbarous words. But rumours whispered of an Arthur weeping and full of pitiful complaints, of an Arthur living with no comfort, of an Arthur dead from fever, from a fall from the battlements, from the bitter pain of his wounds. Men in Brittany tolled bells to mourn his passing and the rumours spread to Paris and Poitiers.

But there was solid news from England, from Corfe Castle, of twenty-five of the French knights there, starved to death. No ransom asked for, just submission, and when they tried to escape, and gained the keep, all food supplies cut off. Isabella listened in horror as John told her this news, her face turned away from his mean triumph.

'I think we can consider the Lusignans now. We perhaps need some reconciliation with those counts and lords south of the Loire. They would be helpful there, as des Roches and Thouars have disrupted so much. And they will swear an oath to remain loyal after their imprisonment. That will have shown them how strong I can be.'

And John laughed at Isabella's face, as she searched to see if he was telling the truth. He was.

'Go, tell Agnes – she will be pleased. She enjoyed that hilltop castle and the small life you had there.'

Isabella walked away quickly, flattered to be told something, trusted to give the news to others.

'He has released Hugh and his brother, but they will not stay faithful to him – the only man who did that was my father. He sealed the marriage alliance with two treaties: one public, the other private. There were secrets between him and John, and he stayed a steady ally. He was always against the rebellious Lusignans. I do not know what will happen now.'

'He has given the Poitevins some leaders once more. The hostility had its head cut off and now John has revived it.'

149

Agnes was right, and they both knew that another storm would break around them soon.

Philippe heard the news of Lusignans freed, and their broken promises to John. Full of contempt for John's perfidy, they joined de Thouars and des Roches. William des Roches was the man who could make a difference in the Poitevin heart-lands and leave Philippe to concentrate elsewhere.

'Rebels on both banks of the Loire, that will keep John and his knights busy, and the Bretons are all stirred up by Arthur's capture and shameful imprisonment – breathing fire, they say. They look to another, more hopeful future with a young prince and a free, glorious Brittany.'

Philippe listened carefully. A free Brittany was something he was not so eager to see, but the prospect of des Roches taking care of Angers, riding with the Lusignans – that was altogether more pleasing.

'You are free, my liege, to attack the Norman borders near Paris: Conches, Bonneville and Gaillard. Now there is a prize!'

John saw how serious it had become, and so quickly too – there was war on all fronts. He ordered stores to be collected and mustered men as fast as he could; a full-scale campaign was brewing. He must try to mend the cracks in the alliance against Philippe, a king now rattling at the Angevin empire. Argentan was the place to be, central Normandy, a good focus with all the roads meeting there. The silver market of the Vikings, and important to the English kings, almost as important as Rouen. It was another town where his father had built a castle, the River Orne nearby providing a bound-ary line.

Christmas in Chinon was quiet, and celebrated without too much ceremony. John could hardly spend time there when he needed to be further north, so as soon as the New Year came in he left for Argentan.

'I will send word when it is safe for you to travel again. I am to dine with the Count of Alençon on Twelfth Night. Robert of Alençon is a fool, so we will mark well the feast of fools! And we can play the fool when we are together again, Isabella, be foolish and fond.'

He stroked her hair and kissed her, whispering loving words, and Isabella thought, is it possible that he loves me? That beneath all the lust and determination to be my master he is entranced by me, that he is willing to be foolish and fond with me?

'You are the Duchess of the Normans, of the men of Aquitaine and of Anjou. You are my beloved queen, my heart's queen.'

And with these words, which left her breathless but happy, he was gone. Conscious of her position, she walked with great dignity back into the castle. She was the Queen Isabella.

And Aimery de Thouars knew this, and as soon as John was many miles away to the north, he struck, besieging Chinon, pressing hard at the castle's defences. Isabella and Agnes sat on the floor of the bedchamber, listening to the shouts of the soldiers as they began to build scaling ladders to climb over the outer walls. Arrows were being fired at them and stones hurled at the marauders.

'Messengers have been sent to John, he will rescue me as he did his mother. He can travel fast when a queen is in danger and I am his queen – he will come with soldiers and I will not be captured by de Thouars. He would ransom me for too many advantages, and I am too valuable to John as a wife and a queen to be taken captive.'

Isabella was flushed and frightened. She needed reassurance that all would be well, that the man who seemed to care for her at last in some true way would arrive, and that she would be safe.

A man did arrive, but not John – a detachment of mercenaries with a Peter de Préaux at their head swept into Chinon, pushed away the troops and within two days had found a roundabout route back to safety in Le Mans, dodging and swerving. De Préaux made sure he could get Isabella to where a frantic John waited for her.

'The roads were impassable, I set out to rescue you but after we passed through Alençon, we heard the news. That great fool – I only dined with him two days previously, that pissing fool of a count – has gone over to Philippe. I could only get as far as Le Mans. I have enemies on all sides.'

Isabella looked at him with some scorn; she had been fearful but so sure that John would be resolute, not cowering away. Yes, he was relieved that she was here and safe, but where was his courage? This indecision, this dithering – what use was his restless energy now?

'My lady, do not worry. We have many castles, great fortified castles, and by the faith that I owe you I know a place, a safe place where you will have protection from the King of France and all his power for ten years and more.' He was holding her hand as he said this, as much to calm himself as to placate Isabella.

'A safe place? Sire, it seems to me that you are a king seeking the corner square where you will be checkmated.'

John raged at her and flung himself around the room, punching the walls with his fists. He stood in front of her, wild eyed, besotted. 'I will not leave you to be undefended again, Isabella. I will stay by your side at all times. Come here, be with me – you know you are my heart's desire.'

They left hurriedly for Rouen, the Norman capital with its great castle and keep. Rouen was to be their refuge now that the Loire had become slippery with treachery. The treasurers' chests and exchequer were being packed up and loaded too. John bit his knuckles watching the trunks being strapped into carts. He needed this money.

The preparations for a spring offensive had been made but John was more often late in bed with Isabella. No counterattacks against Philippe were ordered; crumbling walls in the stronghold castles were not repaired, and began to fall down. John flitted from Isabella's bed to Caen, to Chinon and back again. Still restless and indecisive, he heard of Philippe taking a boat down the river to Saumur where he encouraged the Poitevin rebels, attacking the heart of Aquitaine.

'I am trapped here in Normandy! They say I am Softsword twice over. Well, we will see how soft I am – I have ordered Arthur to be brought here, to be closely guarded in the new tower. With a new man to keep watch – Hubert de Burgh has displeased me. He has been too lenient with that unloved nephew.'

Arthur arrived, to be kept by a new jailer; someone whom John hoped would not defy him and would be a harsh guardian. William de Briouze had been at Mirebeau, a fierce fighter, and it was de Briouze who had captured Arthur and had expected him to be released to des Roches as promised. That would perhaps have eased John's conscience, but his conscience did not trouble him. In this de Briouze felt close to his king, a more constant companion than many. Rapacious and ruthless in all his work, he was known to have killed three Welsh princes in a massacre at a Christmas feast. A jailer for Arthur with dirty hands.

Isabella saw the slight, fair-headed youth dismount. About my age, about fifteen, she realised as she watched him being shuffled into the tower, and then into the dungeon. She turned away from the window and concentrated on unpacking and repacking the treasure chests. Here were the crown jewels, an amazing crown that Matilda had brought with her from Germany, heavy gold, so heavy it needed silver rods to support it. A great gold cross and huge ruby sat in the centre. A smaller crown, decorated in gold flowers, grander and more precious than Isabella's small guirland but like that piece, delicate and feminine. Many gold goblets, silver plate, gold coins. A golden wand with a dove, and the extraordinary sword of Tristram, with its message of honour and justice and mercy down the length of the blade. John had ordered a tally to be made of all the contents, and had allowed her some responsibility. So she counted and tallied and Agnes rechecked, and they both kept very quiet.

John was fretful again; the war was not to his liking. He lacked the energy to make the decisions needed, fingers pointed and his enemies' nicknames Lackland, Softsword were whispered everywhere. Isabella had goaded him, calling him a check-mated king, but together they had turned the bedchamber into a place of long, passionate days; he could not stop fondling, caressing and exploring her body, his fingers paddled in her secret softness until they were both exhausted. The nights were for drinking bouts. He was worn out, slumped in his chair, cup after cup of wine called for and then hastily tipped down, followed by a prowl around the room, biting his nails and swearing.

'I need to bolster my trust in the lords and counts but it is hard, the Lusignans all forfeited and they do mischief. The men in the south turned against me, they fear me and loathe me. Such despair I have. I will strike again, I will.'

And he ordered a boat to be made ready, to sail down the Seine to his manor at Molineux, a place of some calm with its three mills, their wheels beating the rushing water. He commanded de Briouze to come with him, as well as three officials who had been trying to get him to sign papers. They knew how he sent secret messages with his signature so that the contents of the letter were countermanded as long as the reader knew the code. This had confused many, and John himself forgot the codes he had set up. Their attempts to sort out this system had led to more petulant outbursts.

'Come with me to where we can think straight. I cannot be worried now about this petty matter – we will be quiet and thoughtful in time for Easter and enjoy the April spring. You can record any cryptic signs I need for my messages to be truly secret.'

De Briouze listened with doubt to this. It was unlike John to talk of being quiet and thoughtful before a religious festival, especially Easter. He worried away at Peter de Mauley, closer to the king now than before, surly but loyal, another Poitevin encouraged into the circle.

'He has said several times, when the drink has been in charge of his tongue, rough words like "What do the priests mean? On Good Friday you can put many gods in the sepulchre but on Easter Day they cannot arise by themselves unless you lift them by the arm and carry them out. And if you do not, they will stay there, in their graves." His soul is full of blasphemies.'

De Mauley listened, and laughed. 'He is always plotting something. Are you scared for your own skin? Then write to him and hand Arthur over to John. He and I can play a game or two with that nephew of his.'

Shaking his head, de Briouze sent for his clerk. 'I do not want any part of it.'

I know not what fate awaits your nephew, whose faithful guardian I have been. I return him to your hands in good health and sound in all his members. Put him, I pray you, in some other, happier custody. The burden of my own affairs bids me resign.

John scowled and laughed as he read the letter.

'I take you at your word, William de Briouze. You can soon return to the burden of your own affairs – you have a family and much land to occupy you.' And then he called de Mauley to come to the table to gamble with him, and sent for de Briouze, who was intent on writing to his wife. 'But stay until the morning. We will take that boat later – the Seine is in full flood tonight. Now stay with me. Drink some more of this wine, we have enough to fill the river and it is good wine.'

'I fear it is the wine of violence.' But de Briouze said this in a low voice towards the open window.

'And I think we can ask Arthur, Prince of Brittany to join us too.'

De Mauley, wrapped in a cloak trimmed with wolfskin, whistled to the hunting dogs as he came back from ordering Arthur to be brought up. They ranged alongside him, eager for some prey.

'The boy is all skin and fear, blue in his face – we cannot let him stay so frightened in this world. He is like deer caught in a thicket, that Breton prince.'

Eyes bleary, face red and enraged, John was lurching around the table to grab at another pitcher of wine and then to grab Arthur, sitting fearful outside the door, held fast by chains. A sword, sharp, out of its scabbard; a blade marked with twelve brass crosses, wrought iron, a steel cutting edge and all its length covered in blood; a boy six times stabbed.

De Briouze stood, 'Call off the dogs de Mauley, they would attack the body.'

His voice was low as he watched in dread to see what would happen next.

'My lord, can this be? This drunken rage has caused a murderous deed; the death of a nephew, a Prince cut down, the King is mad with wine, bedevilled.'

De Mauley turned the body over, and pushed his blade

into the heart. Then he called to de Briouze to help and they dragged Arthur out of the door and into the boat. John stumbled after them.

'We are but ten miles from Molineux and the mill-wheels.'

On the bank of the river they found great stones, heavy stones, for here were the mills that ground the wheat and stones had been left. And here was rope for tying the sacks of flour, and here was Arthur, tied to a granite weight and cast into the Seine.

'He was possessed of the Devil, and no man can speak of it or write of it. Some say that fishermen discovered the body, the head crushed by rocks, and dragged it in their nets and Arthur was buried, in secret, near the priory of Bec, Notre Dame des Prés. The Angevin rage, that drunken rage that catches hold, it could be possible?'

Agnes twisted her skirt nervously as she related the story that she had been told. Isabella was looking out of the window to where she had seen Arthur for the first and last time.

'Philippe keeps saying, "First produce Arthur" when John tries to negotiate some peace treaty, but he cannot be found. In Brittany they will not forgive his disappearance – they have condemned the English king as a murderer. But I have to forgive him, for I have to live with him as his wife and queen.'

The song, the lay, the lament was sung throughout the southwest and the words carried on the early summer breeze, into open doors, through windows, and no one stopped their ears or put a hand across the singer's mouth.

The English king Lackland
Has Arthur by ambush taken
Slain by the English king's sword

157

Is Arthur into the Seine cast
Alas! Alas! Play the music
All Brittany is mourning today
For here drowned a prince
Arthur, in his sixteenth year of life
The Seine is red with blood.

And John lay next to Isabella, entwined in her arms, covering her with kisses and caresses, unable to leave her alone. He was careless of the world outside the bedchamber, helpless before the lust that engulfed him.

Isabella was triumphant, she conjured and delighted him; cajoled him into spending all his time with her. She slithered her bewitching body on his, claimed him with her mouth and rose to meet him in an ecstasy.

All around men gossiped and told tales.

'She has the makings of a witch, an animal more than a queen.'

'Their appetites know no bounds. When I told him that the King of France had taken another castle and dragged off the castellans tied to horses' tails, men who had been loyal to John and defending the English property, he just said, "Let it be, let it be." And then he said, "Whatever he now takes, I will one day recover."'

'And when Vaudreuil simply surrendered! Such a vital link in the chain, full of provisions and men and armaments, and they just opened the gates to Philippe! John has written that he ordered the surrender and there was no blame attached to anyone.'

'Ha! They sing of its glorious defence and make rude signs when they do so.'

'But we still have Rouen, and Château Gaillard will be impossible to defeat. It defends us always. Richard built it to be untakeable.'

*

But Philippe was getting ready to challenge this place, and his siege engine was advancing up to Gaillard. It had mocked the French kings for long enough.

John prowled around the chamber in his dressing gown and Isabella smiled at him from the pillows. But there was no falling back into her arms this time; at last he was full of energy and scheming.

'This is where I take back what is ours, Isabella. I am not unnerved by this fresh assault. I have plans, I have a focus, and we will not allow Philippe to punch us so hard.'

Troops mustered to break the siege, a clever plan of how to run supplies through the blockade, a bold night operation, the river and boats, a naval detachment, a force of men from Flanders, William Marshall would take an army of knights and foot soldiers and the land force would take the French where they camped on the banks of the Seine while the naval force would smash the pontoon.

Despair. Everything went wrong and the French repulsed every attack on land. The naval force was lost and the river ran with their blood. John cursed that no one had been able to follow through his plans, turned away and made a swift decision to throw himself across Normandy, to crush the Bretons, to draw Philippe away from Gaillard, still besieged but not taken. He was making desperate moves, the last desperate moves of an English king in Normandy. Gaillard must not fall.

The English castellans who were dogged and loyal, who were not tempted by French offers, worried away at the problems; English dominance crumbling, England wavering and weak. This was not what they were used to, they were used to sending French kings fleeing to back to the safety of Paris but now Normandy was nearly overrun, and a French victory was near. 'It is a year of shame.'

'Nothing he does helps to save our defences from collapsing.'

'Too many knights and barons have gone over to Philippe. Treachery runs through Normandy like a plague.'

And John railed against the treachery and could not bear to hear the men, who said, 'He can bring no help to those besieged because all the time he fears his subjects' treason.'

'Their hearts are lost, and they have too many miles to cover, too many fiefdoms to control, and he is so mean and cruel, a vicious man.'

'Since the death of Richard there has been no leadership, and now he turns to mercenaries as there are scant few knights to serve him. The people do not love him.'

And the mercenaries, the wolves, ran through Normandy, pillaging as if in enemy territory, filling their pockets with the profits of any office thrown their way and taking everything they could from estates and tenants. English treasure, silver coin arrived, shipped across the Channel to pay the castle guards, and not once but twice the money had to be sent for. In Falaise John sent carts of silver out to the camps.

'I must give land to some for services. We have no more money to pay for knights, indeed we do not have knights, just young warriors not yet sworn to fealty. We need them for an armed escort, I fear to move without them. I must take this strange route back to Rouen, all others seem dangerous to me – straight they may be, but full of enemies. And I must get back to the queen – I said I would not leave her again.'

Rouen was a haven, well-fortified, an island of safety but encircled, and Gaillard was still under siege. The treason that fed John's mind worked away at him. He wanted to strike, but where?

Isabella was learning how he played upon hopes and fears

of all around him, and how loyalty vanished when a king's malevolence struck hard.

'You have too few friends. A challenge to your enemies will cripple you.'

'Are you afraid? Then flee like a rabbit – I shall not go for a year. No, I shall stay here for Christmas, take in the New Year. I need to write to my mother tell her of some of these things, what is going forward with us.'

And hearing this, Isabella felt that she was listening to bold talk that hid great panic. She knew this man so much better now than three years ago when he had married her in Angoulême. He who trusted no one was distrusted by all the world.

XIV

John was ordering the packhorses and carts to be readied. Isabella had been told to buy cloth from the merchants who were making their way from Flanders further south. Agnes helped her choose. It was English wool, woven by the Flemish weavers and dyed with skill.

'The sanguine is a good strong colour, and they have fixed it well with alum.'

Agnes fingered the bolts of cloth and approved of what she found. Isabella bought a good length of the red wool, thinking how cheerful it would be for Christmas, and then chose some new linen cloth mixed with silk. It was very expensive but she only wanted enough for a new chemise. John hardly glanced at the purchases; he was explaining his movements to William Marshall, who listened with grave attention, thinking that this was a story he did not want to hear.

'We will visit England for a short while and seek help from my barons there. There may be some wise counsel they can give. Then we will return at once to Rouen. Immediately return, you understand?'

The baggage carts were sent ahead, well-guarded. John feasted and nervously joked for a couple of days after they rumbled away towards the coast, and then told Marshall to be ready to ride to Caen. It was an anxious, jangly ride out. They slept the first night in a small town, fearful, and looking over their shoulders all the time.

'I hear that my barons swear to hand me over to Philippe. Well, I dismiss this idea – such treachery is not to be believed, but here in the town, not in the castle, I am safer. There are no barons to concern us, and no one in the town dare speak out.'

Isabella curled up tight in their bed; he had said they would leave before daybreak. She had told Agnes to be ready for an early departure – no need to undress tonight.

But at midnight they were riding again; he had hardly slept and gripped her hand while they lay side by side before hissing at her, 'Come, we leave now. We are supposed to be sleeping but we will press on in the dark. I trust no one.'

'I must wake Agnes.'

'No, she will stay here in France – no more of your countrywomen this time, we have enough trouble getting to the ship without arousing suspicions. Agnes can go home.'

'No! How can you tell me this? You are too cruel.'

He twisted her arm high behind her back. 'Make haste and do as I say.'

'I need to tell her this! I must take her leave, say farewell – she has no one to help her here in Normandy.'

'Be quiet. There is no time.' And John pushed her out into the cold December night and they rode like demons, miles through the night; seven miles, twenty miles, Caen, then Bayeux where they stopped to rest. The next day at Barfleur some had managed to catch up with them and farewells were made, with impatience from John and misgivings from his men. When would they see their king again?

We fight our own shadows forever, thought Isabella, low and dispirited as once more she crossed the Channel for England.

The court at Canterbury was celebrating Christmas with gusto, even though the news from France was that there were threats all along the valley of the Seine, all those defensive castles beset by Philippe and treason. John needed money to make a show of strength, to steer the Norman barons back to his side.

'It is in their interests to have land in Normandy under the English king and land here too. The greatest of them have such holdings they could almost be kings themselves! It will take time but I am not about to abandon the fight.'

Strong words said from the comfort of the hall as he watched the dancing, drinking warm spiced wine, Isabella by his side in a blood-red wool dress, long and full but tight at the waist, tied with a needlework belt, its silver gilt buckle bright in the candlelight. The high neck of the dress was cut open at the front but closed again with a brooch. Her Christmas gift. The goldsmith had arrived as soon as he knew that John was in Canterbury, hoping to be summoned, knowing how much the king liked jewellery. John had not stinted on buying for himself even though the money was needed for his campaign. He saw the look on Isabella's face as she took in the glittering show.

'I might be well disposed to gift you a piece. A reward, my queen, for all your fond attentions.'

Sharp words came into her mind, words about him discarding Agnes and leaving Isabella with scant women around her, and no dowry lands or income yet. And Angoulême, hers but not hers. But he spread the brooches out in front of her: the twists of gold with their pearl and opal flowers, the beaten silver oval holding a smooth red ruby, a ring brooch, its own circle punctuated with smaller circles, each one filled with a small sapphire.

'I would be happy with this one.' Isabella picked it up and held it to her lips. 'It feels so hard and so smooth.' Her look was knowing, and the tip of her tongue flicked. And now she wore it, fastening her dress against any draughts.

The dancers swirled and finished in front of the dais where Isabella and John sat on the two carved oak chairs. As the music finished John crowed and called for more dancing, and indicated that Isabella would join in the next dance, another carole.

Holding hands with all the others in the circle, Isabella felt free and full of joy. They were singing as they danced clockwise, and as the leader called out they stamped their feet. John watched and gloated: she was still young and slim with narrow hips and high breasts, but knew how to be a woman now. A woman that he could own completely, and surely soon there would be babies? An heir, a legitimate heir – he had enough bastard children: more than a dozen, for whom he had happily provisioned. He remembered them all, and their mothers; some were high-born wives and daughters, and it was always good to remind a fine lady that she was the same as any other wench when it came to the games played in bed. Anyway, there were plenty of Fitzroys, sons of the king, but no heir to his throne yet. Hawisa, his first wife, ten years and no children, she seemed happy enough in her own way, so she might be useful if Isabella became difficult or contrary. A reminder that he could cast a wife aside if necessary.

The dance had stopped and the gathered throng looked to him to see what was wanted now.

'Another dance, a couples' dance. Come, let us make pairs and this time I will join you all.'

A rustling of skirts and some cleared a space for John, many of the ladies anxious not to hold his hand or feel his lecherous touch. They need not have worried – it was with Isabella that he wanted to trace patterns on the floor, a musical prelude.

In their bedchamber he undressed her slowly, lingering over the untying of her girdle, letting the rich wool of her skirt fall to the ground in folds and crumples. He undid the circle brooch, and lifted her tunic over her head.

'You have enjoyed this Christmas, I believe. Last year was dismal as we waited for war to begin – here we are more peaceful and we can lie abed again.'

She stood in the new fine linen and silk chemise, thin shoulder straps slipping down. Her hair was unpinned and her eyes glowed with excitement as she reached out a hand to John and led him to the bed.

'We will dance again, you and me, a slow pavanne and then something faster.'

'You must leap to me and for me – it is only when the woman feels herself trembling inside that a seed can be fertile. I want you to tremble tonight.'

And so the holiday was spent, a feast of lust and passion with Isabella now matched to all desires. If Normandy was to be lost, it was lost under the bed canopy of the king.

This year, Epiphany meant a visit to Oxford; the barons needed to be told that they must pay up for a new campaign in France. Normandy had to be rescued from Philippe.

A year ago John had breakfasted with Robert Alençon and been betrayed by him within the day, and he shuddered as he recalled that time. It took a few weeks and hard words to persuade the barons to dig deep in their coffers to find the marks needed to buy more mercenaries; it appeared that everyone was scraping together the money. Supplies were being gathered and sent across the Channel and John sighed with relief; the plan was working and he would have the resources behind him for an overwhelming counterattack from the south. There would be good hunting in Normandy.

As all was being made ready, there came the worst possible news. Gaillard, the fortress château that protected Rouen, had been taken by Philippe. The six months of siege were over.

'How can this be?! The great stone cliffs were strong, high, and the defenders determined, able, loyal men.'

The messenger knelt with a bowed head. How to begin? 'The men were strong and brave inside Gaillard. No blame to them – they lost very few and killed many of the attackers.'

'And the provisions, they were not starved out? All civilians had been sent away, the food and water was only for the fighting men.'

'This is true, indeed there was no starvation or surrender. The castle fell like this – it came about in the following way...'

A hesitation, and an impatient gesture from John.

'The French king had men who sheltered under the stone ledge that crossed the moat, and they sat there protected from arrows and chipped and chipped at the foundations of the keep.'

'Mice nibbling at the walls? This would not bring them down.'

'The men inside could not get to them to harry them, so they burrowed out and scared them off. That was good – they forced them away from the shelter of the bridge.'

John was black in the face with rage, leaning on his hand to one side of the chair, biting his lips and snarling.

'This burrowing in and out made the wall weak in places, and that was when they brought in the huge trebuchet, slinging great stones at the wall until it collapsed. The great wall near the bridge was breached. A hundred and fifty-six men were left alive to surrender.'

'Philippe told my brother Richard when he built the castle that even if the walls were made of iron he would take it, and by the throat of God, he has.'

What now? A time of emergency talks with the many barons, appeals to the Pope, archbishops and bishops – all were anxious that these two warring kings should make peace and both go to the Holy Land. A crusade was necessary to salve their souls, which had been so blackened by this fighting.

Philippe sat in Paris and considered his soul as the delegation entreated him, and told him that John was ready for peace.

'I will certainly make peace, as soon as John releases Prince Arthur to me and to his Breton fiefdoms. And if he cannot find Arthur, who has been silent now for twelve months, then his sister Eleanor, the Fair Maid of Brittany whom I believe is in England at Corfe Castle. She should be in her own country I would see her at the court in Paris. And all John's possessions in this country will be forfeit – we cannot have the Angevin kings of England lording it so close to our capital, guarding the way to the Channel coast and the way to the south of our lands.'

Another year of skirmish, another year of pointless discussions, another year of brooding on how to defend and retake Norman land, or how to conquer all of it.

In Fontevraud Eleanor lay in her bed, not speaking to any of her servants or commanding letters to be written by her secretary. The news of the fall of Gaillard, built by her favourite son and then lost by the most treacherous of them all, had seen her bowed down and weakened. Her hands were quiet and still on the quilt, its thick patchwork covering such a frail body. She died on an April spring morning and was buried at Fontevraud, a glorious effigy over her tomb, which was placed between those of her husband and her son. Her ladies wrote of how good and noble she was, but many remembered her as that giddy, fearless, defiant woman who had become a skilled negotiator and ruler, but a true Poitevin. Her secretary paid for Masses to be said for her and spoke to the abbess before he slipped away to Poitiers.

'She was woven into the story of the Angevins, and the Aquitaine was woven into her. And now she is gone,

Aquitaine will not look to John with the same respect.'

Philippe knew this, and planned to send mercenaries there to join William des Roches and the Lusignans and take it all. The Poitou and then Angoulême.

But first there was the matter of Normandy. He swung his forces south of Rouen and drove up through Falaise and Caen, which surrendered without a murmur. Homage was hastily made by townspeople and barons. It was safe to desert to Philippe now, and besides, the loyalty to John had withered long ago. And the Bretons joined him at Caen, still full of the fire of revenge for Arthur. The Cherbourg peninsula and the castles of the south-eastern borders of Normandy surrendered, and now Philippe advanced, advanced, advanced, while Rouen waited.

'My lord, we have news that the archives from Caen have been brought across to Shoreham.'

A nervous message to John, who sat biting his nails, always biting his nails, and twitching.

'Well, do not wait – send some carts to collect them, we will have them here in London. What other news is there?'

'Philippe has confirmed all the civic liberties granted to Rouen – all those trading privileges you gave them are still theirs. He has guaranteed them.'

'I am sure he has! Such loyalty! Well trade away, my fine citizens, and see if you are the only town that Philippe so blesses.'

And Philippe granted several towns special status, making sure that the Rouennais knew that their top-dog position was being undermined, as Gaillard had been.

Another message, this time from the commander of the English forces in Rouen.

'Peter de Préaux has agreed a truce with Philippe, an armistice. He wishes to save the destruction of the city. He says that without an army to relieve the city he stands no chance. But he has said that he will hold out for thirty days, and only then, if there is no help from his king, will he surrender.'

'This is the third time I have been told this. No help can be looked for from me – everyone must do what they think best.'

John sank further into his chair. All was lost, Normandy was lost and there was no hope to be had.

Mutterings at court in London; mutterings in Rouen.

'Richard had the heart of the Normans, John has nothing except distrust. Richard would have been on the heights commanding an attack, he would have been in Rouen with his sword, ready to fight.'

'John enjoys every kind of pleasure with his queen, and thinks that all he has to do is find enough money and buy back the lands he lost, the lands his father and brother won so ably.'

'For Richard the Normans were willing to take on all risks, he was a king who made the fight seem won before it had begun.'

'Now they are like chaff, blown this way and that – no leadership, only panic.'

Isabella was scornful in their chamber, listening to the news of the defeat and the loss of such rich territory.

'Philippe is already pulling down the castle in Rouen and building his own citadel – it is as if you had never been. And he is saying that your men are dirty rags, soiled by the latrine.'

John grabbed her by her hair and hissed, 'Listen, my lady, I have lost everything for you.'

Isabella, head back, held tight, snapped back, 'Sire, I lost the best knight in the world for you.'

John tugged on her hair and almost spat. 'You still hanker after the Lusignan? Well, I should not have freed him – he and his brothers did not serve me well. But Philippe will ride down there soon I think, and then we will see what happens to Angoulême.'

And he flung her on the bed, pushing up her skirts.

'You are to be breached, Isabella, your citadel will fall again and again, and you cannot deny any battering that comes at you.'

She fought back, scratching at his face, pushing at him and turning away from him. He laughed.

'Like that, my lady? So be it. The church does not care for coupling like curs, but we know better, we can make the beast with two backs. This is a place where I am not a Softsword.'

XV

Gloucester Castle, December 1214

Isabella gazed out of the window at the castle meadows. John had made sure she was here with the children, a place of sanctuary. She had come here for the birth of Isabelle, and Henry and Richard were here too; all the children, to keep them safe from kidnapping. To keep her safe, he said, to keep the children safe.

The last ten furious years had been difficult and troubled. Isabella was always frustrated, unable to assert herself as she wanted; constantly sent off to one castle or another. She understood that this was how their life was to be, and with the children and the pregnancies she had accepted it. But no court of her own and no income kept her away from where the decisions were made. She had wanted and expected influence, like Eleanor.

And now John had arrived, riding furiously from where to where? So much turmoil in England and he did not bother her with his plans. She was pleased to see that he cared enough to visit and see his new daughter, and he had paid the wet nurse well. But when would she see him again, and how could she be sure of any power while he fought with the barons and the French, and she had no influence with either?

'Why am I not paid my dowry income? You grant me

these lands in France and England but do I see any of the gold coming to me? You wish to keep me powerless, falsely confirming that I am to have this or that town or county so that others think me well provided for, but I am like your first wife, dependent. You give my dower lands to others if this suits your plans. I am forever left with nothing.'

John watched her storming around the nursery, and jeered. 'I buy jewels for you, my lady, when I am in the mood for giving you a token or two.'

'And many more for yourself! Such a treasure you have collected. Hundreds of rings set with sapphires and diamonds. I should have learnt from the example of Berengaria, eternally and vainly pleading for her inheritance. You do not treat crowned queens with honour, you cheat them. She was destitute!'

'She seems to be happy enough now. A few months in her sister's court, living so close with kin, made them both realise they had some strategic land and property to bargain with.'

'Yes, and she swore allegiance to Philippe because you refused all her entreaties. She had to have something of her own, and at least he gave her 1,000 marks, an award she needed.'

'And do not forget he gave her Le Mans too, one of my towns. Well, she can have it – it is so battered and broken-down, it will serve her well enough. I hear she is busy building an abbey – perhaps that is something you might consider one day? But I think you are not so holy, my queen whom they call Jezebel.'

More jeers, laughter, a quick, fierce embrace, and kisses. She protested as he pulled her away from children, babies, wet nurses, and into the chamber where he thrust her onto the bed. Her protests were stopped with hard hands as he jostled and pulled at her shift, nuzzling her with a greedy mouth.

'This is better than we remember my lady, my unholy

queen who has sometimes dallied where she should not. Do not think I have forgotten the man who should by all that swives be haunting this room. Or indeed your half-brother, who has perhaps offered you more than safe shelter.'

Isabella hissed back, 'And do not think I have forgotten Maud Fitzwalter.' But her mouth was stopped with a rough hand and he took her so quickly and fiercely that she sobbed throughout. And then he was gone, and Isabella was left in a mess of bed linen and dishevelled skirts, her hair pulled about and her face wet with tears. She sank back, defeated.

This bed had been marked by tumult before, and ended with horror. It had begun with so much admiration and attention: her feverish flirting with a young knight bachelor had been exciting and her skills in bed had educated him well. He had been the son of a man the King wanted to keep under control, a hostage of sorts, sent by the John to be part of her small retinue. She found she enjoyed the authority that experience gave her and looked forward to their encounters, careless who knew of or heard the noisy, exuberant lovemaking. John had flaunted his affairs; she saw no reason to dissemble.

And then he had discovered what she was doing and casually, so very casually and with a malicious cruelty, had castrated the man and hung his body at the end of her bed. He had laughed in her face when she pulled back the bed-hangings and saw the swinging shape, waiting eagerly for her response because he liked to see the hurt he caused. And he had always enjoyed recalling it and forcing her to remember. The pity of it all was that there was no pity.

And if I am not holy, thought Isabella, as she pinned up her hair, then you, my lord, are the least devout man I have ever met. For John had made trouble, trouble with the Pope over the appointment of the new Archbishop of Canterbury, and a papal interdict had hit the religious communities and the good, pious people of England hard. No Mass, no baptisms, no burials, so there had been such stinking sights, horrible to see, in the ditches outside the towns; the church doors sealed, no celebration or feasting on the saints' days, and everyone feeling abandoned by their king who was known for his heretical ways. He was always making offerings to atone for hunting or eating meat on Fridays. He joked about it too: 'See how fat that stag has grown without ever attending Mass!'

Not only heretical but cruel, aggressive and full of revenge for any he considered a threat to his power and authority.

She shuddered. The worst memories were of the de Briouze family; somehow their lives mixed up with the death of Prince Arthur, a disappearance that no one referred to now. Not even Philippe seemed to care about the fate of the young man he had knighted and set on John.

John's friendship with de Briouze had cooled; he was no longer a favoured companion, for as his power grew, John began to detest him as he detested all powerful men. And de Briouze was not only lord of much of the south of Wales, he also had Limerick in Ireland. Rewarded by John, but not trusted by John. William knew about Arthur and owed John money, and John chased him for it. And John chased William's wife Matilda, sending messengers demanding her sons as hostages. It was told that de Briouze had begged her to hold her tongue, but her reply had been defiant.

'I will not deliver up my sons as hostages to your lord, King John, because where is his nephew who was his ward? Arthur's fate shows what happens to boys kept in his custody, which should be honourable but which proved not.'

De Briouze was red and white with anger and fear as her answer echoed back to him.

'You have spoken out of turn, like a stupid woman, I was ready, I am ready to make amends. I was going to make amends…that was rash, Matilda. We will pay for those words, however true they be.'

175

He turned out to be a cowardly man, William de Briouze, who fled with his family to Ireland and then on to Scotland, where betrayal caught them all. But William escaped to France, in some despair and with some guilt hanging over him. Proud, saucy Matilda and her eldest boy were thrown into the prison in Windsor Castle and were found dead, starved, their pathetic bodies twisted into grim shapes.

Not to be thought about, or dwelt upon. Isabella shook her head against the images of the scene that had been described to all in grim whispers.

'Matilda died holding her son. He had died first, but she had eaten at his cheeks in her despair and hunger.'

It was for such deeds that John was hated by the barons. That and heavy taxes and the loss of Normandy; that rich place lost, and all its wealth with the French king now. The domains that so many had owned, forfeited. And John had spent all the years afterwards in England, worrying over every detail that he could, insisting on records being kept and watching expenditure. And now the barons were determined that he would obey some legislation to check his unfair demands. She felt relieved that she had so often been far from London or Oxford or York while all the trouble swirled around him.

She stood up and called for a basin of water to wash. Would news come of successful talks about this difficult business, news that John had managed to stop the barons, his enemies, the king's enemies? Would his nerve hold? Such trouble there had been with the barons after the disastrous Battle of Bouvines last year, when all was lost in France. Philippe had been triumphant; he had managed what he had always wanted: to drive the English out of France. The French were beginning to forge a nation at last.

In the nursery she found Henry, and folded him into a tight embrace. The heir to England, just turned seven, slim and pale, not stocky like his father. He was kind too, and loving – she minded that she did not see so much of him now he had been sent to live most of the time in Winchester with the bishop, Peter des Roches, so well advanced by John to that rich position. Well, if Henry was to be prepared for a life as a king, des Roches was an able teacher, not only a bishop but treasurer and Archdeacon of Poitiers. She ought to like and trust him more, he was wealthy and influential and he knew the Poitevin, but there was something harsh in the way he regarded Isabella. She shook her head – bitter thoughts – and pushed Henry away from her, her impatience spilling over.

John's absurd accusations had made her discontented and anxious. Veiled accusations of incest with her half-brother – it sounded like monkish gossip. Peter de Joigny had been someone to trust, faithful and trustworthy; rare commodities in the English court. Had not John invited him to England when she was pregnant with Henry, writing that she greatly desired to see him? There were no countrywomen in her circle of attendants and she had felt so lost and troubled, living with John's first wife. A friendly face with news about Angoulême, and letters from her mother that were much desired indeed. He was welcomed at court and she remembered the few visits he managed to make with fondness.

And had not Peter joined them in Poitou last year against the French? Risking his estates in Burgundy to support John, and acting as a witness to several charters and documents. She wondered if she would see him again; he had always offered kind words and the promise of safety. And straightforward – not like John, who denied her so much: no court of her own as queen consort, promising endowments, even reconfirming them but always there were adjustments.

Adjustments! Some could not make them; Maude

Fitzwalter could not make them, so beautiful, so virtuous. Last year she refused John over and over again, her father rejecting John too. Not like Isabella's father who had connived with him and helped to hand her over to such a lecherous man. No, Robert Fitzwalter had protested, and for this his castle had been sacked and Robert fled to France with his wife and two younger children.

'Mathilda – or Maude, some say, I call her Mathilda.' Terric, her knight, given into her household when she had landed back from France at Dartmouth in the summer, had brought the news to Isabella as she walked heavily in the grounds of Corfe Castle in late October. Already he was a man who could bring her news; often in letters from John, sometimes from gossip from the stable yards and kitchens. 'She was put in the Tower of London, imprisoned right at the top of the turret. Awful place, cold northeast corner, winds very cruel. And a cage in the room, no room to move about.'

Isabella thought of being cold and lonely and walked a little more quickly. John's prisoners were often starved; it appealed to his sense of malevolence. The Poitevin and Breton knights had been starved here, captured after fighting for Arthur and not ransomed, as was the chivalrous custom, but humiliated and starved.

'Mathilda was denied food, very hungry. They say an egg was sent to her, full of poison. She ate it. Famished, she was.'

Isabella reached out a hand and Terric helped her up the stairs to the gate. 'And she died?'

'Yes, she died.' Terric took the letter that had arrived that hour from his jerkin. 'I have orders here, my lady, from the king, written at the Tower of London, for me to take good care of you at this time, and let the king know of your condition.'

And Terric did take good care; he was one of the few men she could trust and rely on. And he had more orders in early

November to take Isabella to Berkhamsted; a slow journey, as she could no longer ride. And then again from there to Gloucester for the birth, to keep her confined in the same bedchamber where Joan, their first daughter, had been born and nursed.

Another lying-in, another daughter, a short confinement and a speedy birth. Pains began just before dawn and by the time the sun was up in the December morning, a daughter had been born. Small and scrawny with dark curls and big eyes, there would be another churching when they would name her Isabelle, a fine new name for an English princess.

At least John had had no more bastard children after their marriage, but he had as many mistresses and women as he wanted; plenty to occupy him in London and Winchester, flaunting his infidelity with whoever caught his eye among the aristocratic ladies at court. Their husbands did not like this poaching of their wives and protested, as they protested against the high taxes, the property tax, the fines levied for the smallest misdeed in the forest law which put obstructions everywhere for both lord and peasant.

'He is intent on pillage. He plunders his subjects, all of us,' was the grumble heard throughout England. 'He had better take care that the people do not forsake him, for his grasping ways are squeezing us all.'

Isabella laughed as she remembered Lady de Neville offering a forfeit of a hundred chickens so that she might spend the night with her husband rather than John, and stopped laughing when she thought of the several times John had sent her to Marlborough Castle, to be looked after by the Nevilles. The home of his sometime mistress.

At least he had not ordered Isabella to live with his first wife again as he had done at the beginning of their marriage; under the same roof as Hawisa in Winchester. She had been ordered to live there, sent to live with his first wife, a bitter retreat for a young bride. John was suspicious of Agnes, the Poitevin maid and companion, mistrusting her influence and gossip. He believed that Hawisa would be a responsible chaperone.

Hawisa seemed resigned, but she was no fool.

'His devious cunning knows no end. I am now, of course, unwed, an unmarried woman with no parents. He tells me that makes me an orphan, an unprotected female in need of a guardian. It is the king's wish to find me a protector. He has made himself that person and I, who was his wife, am now his ward.'

'But he sends you gifts of good cloth, and much wine.'

Isabella always thought that gifts meant more than they did. A strong acquisitive streak had surfaced as she observed the king and his possessions. His rings set with emeralds, sapphires and rubies, his gold flagons, his goblets, all gleaming in chests, safeguarded and gloated over.

'Indeed, and I have an allowance too, but John manages my lands and I have a great inheritance. I have been shunned since you became his wife, shut away here. He will not let me go and it will be to his benefit if I am to wed again. Who will marry me? I am twenty-six and not a young bride like I was, as some are. So I watch and wait with you.'

And then Isabella became pregnant with Henry, and Hawisa was sent to live in Dorset with her allowance cut.

'He is inclined to be mean-natured,' was all that Hawisa had said as she left.

Isabella thought her lucky to ever be married again. To be married for the second time, seven years later, in the year of the Battle of Bouvines when money was needed for the campaign. Lucky to be worth so much. It had been with great delight that John demanded 20,000 marks from Hawisa's new husband. Still no children. She must be barren; rich in some ways, but not in this.

What an angry, lusty, sometimes loving time Isabella and John had made of marriage. Producing four children, all of whom lived. Four children in seven years. There was no doubt that she had a good, strong body, and that John had made use of it.

She wandered over to Henry and patted his head. He smiled up at her; he was always so forgiving of her moods.

The first birth, the first lying-in in Winchester. The room where she had been closeted for days, waiting. The women who had made the cradle ready with soft cloths and given her beakers of a sweet, spicy drink, full of honey and herbs.

Gladys, able and competent, reassuring, reminding her of Agnes. She had poured another drink for Isabella to sip. 'It will soothe the pains as they cramp again.'

Then she had taken one look at Isabella, white-faced and panting, and gently guided her to the bed. Gladys had pushed up her shift and put an ear to her swollen belly.

'You will be delivered by tomorrow. Your baby will be born on the first day of October, a beginning for us all.'

Isabella remembered grasping tight the knotted, silky rope that was tied to the bed for her to grip when the pains washed over her. She groaned, and they had smoothed her hair and washed her face with fresh linen.

The labour had not been too long but there had been waves of pain carrying her backwards and forwards, probing fingers and hands that had reached for a slippery, bloody baby who slithered into the world, gasping for breath but full of vigour and soon bawling, his red face screwed up tight. They had swaddled him and put him in the cradle. She remembered how he had sneezed, and then as he did so, John's anxious words.

'He is well and whole?'

'He is well and whole,' she repeated as Henry began to

cry again, an angry, hungry wail that brought Ellen, his wet nurse, scurrying.

John smiled and took Isabella's hand, stroking her fingers one by one. 'There will be more children. We make strong babies, you and I.'

The choirs had sung anthems for her safe delivery and a boy, an heir. And after him, fifteen months later came Richard, another boy for which all were pleased. He was an Angevin through and through, strong and broad even at five, with a coppery sheen in his hair. Then a girl, born eighteen months after Richard. Joan, not as proud or haughty as Isabella, had been gentle, obedient and meek. A little frightened of her mother, who swooped with flashes of anger when she thought Joan was making too much noise. She had been easily teased by her brothers, not that she saw them now. Joan was away in France with the Lusignans, four years old and betrothed to a man thirty years older. Isabella smiled thinly. Always these betrothals, these alliances, daughters being served up as bonds.

And now the new baby, Isabelle, conceived in France when they had been preparing for the big campaign against Philippe, that expensive and disastrous war.

XVI

In 1214 she had sailed with John to La Rochelle. They had advanced up the Poitevin lands; Isabella determined to show that she could at least be a figurehead for her countrymen, someone to whom shifting loyalties might stick and hold. John had insisted that two of their children come too, so Richard of Cornwall rode with them even though he was only five, and their daughter Joan, a few months before she turned four.

Philippe was watching it all from the borders with the Poitevin, as John made skirmishes and forays out from La Rochelle, even scouring through La Marche, the county that had been given to her father, but was back with the Lusignans again, who were still hostile; who were still angry.

'There is no security here in these fiefdoms of Aquitaine. I would that there were. Poitevins give me no deference and scant loyalty.'

Isabella bit her lip and turned away. The plain truth was that no one trusted John. What was he? He was not a great warrior, not a fighter that men could follow, one that they could boast about, saying, 'Yes, I will ride with my king today.' Indeed, he seemed mostly to bring fear and loathing, as he took so much from all and gave back so little. Isabella had wheedled and flattered to get what she wanted, and had given him pleasure in the bedchamber. And sons, daughters; do not forget the children. She turned back. Was now the time to ask again about more powers for herself, to bring her inherited rights to Angoulême to his attention once more?

But John was smiling at her with malice. 'I think we can afford to be friendly towards the Lusignans again. Your Hugh is married now to your cousin, and we must take heed of that – there is a need to be careful of how that affects any dower lands that might be yours. But I could give them the Saintonge, all that rich land around Saintes, very sweet to own, and Île d'Oléron – good fish and oysters, some nice pickings in tithes and taxes. But your Hugh, old Hugh, now his son is in need of a wife. I have a pleasing thought. I am proposing that we offer our daughter Joan, a nice salve for those old wounds.'

Isabella leapt forward, her hand ready to slap, but was caught by John and tumbled onto the bed.

'Not so fast. Philippe has offered one of his sons in marriage to Joan – do we want an alliance with that deceitful king? We do not, and this will be a good defiance of him and his plans. And now, my lady, I am going to curb your temper in a way that will keep you biddable for me. And take the Lusignans by force if necessary, a battering and a siege on all sides.'

And so he did, intimidating the Lusignans and making sure that all the Poitevin barons witnessed the contract of marriage between Joan and young Hugh, son of Hugh IX, Count of Lusignan, but Isabella did not go to see this ceremony. She lay on her bed and wept; she knew that the seed had quickened again, and that there would be another child.

John was at the Loire, writing that all was good, that Angers was his; the old centre of the Angevins had opened its gates to him. It was important to be at the place where his ancestors had made their home, years ago. John was crowing with delight.

'Send for Isabella and the children. Send for my treasure

– we need the chests of coin and silver. We can move north again.'

Twelve weeks of swift victories followed. His siege train was full of Poitevin barons. He was ready for pitched battle against des Roches, that old friend and enemy, still the lord of the Loire. Des Roches, who was about to be joined by Prince Louis and the French army; a French prince prepared to lead a battle. Time for John to show his mettle and score a decisive victory. How many victories had eluded him? Always treachery dashed his hopes, but now…now he could succeed. Were the Lusignans still with him?

They turned to John and then back to Philippe – what did they want? To make their own secret peace with the French king was always a possibility, and John's spies found letters sent to them by Aimery de Thouars; letters warning Ralph Lusignan that Philippe Augustus intended to come south of the Loire in the first week of September. Aimery wrote:

Make common cause with me. There can be no common cause with John, whom I have asked, in vain, for help to defend my lands against the Capetian king and his army. I have much money that John owes me, all in arrears; I asked for it all to be paid and I asked for knights, crossbowmen and more defences for my castle at Bressuire. John offers only a little and suggests that what he offers will defend both Bressuire and Thouars. I replied that if I were given a truce by the French I would take it. John orders me against taking any such chance. He believes nothing I tell him, whether I tell him good or ill news – he scorns it all. So ride alongside me, lest you lose your head through your tail.

John read the letters and laughed; he would keep the Lusignans on his side and keep his hold over the city of Angoulême. He needed those Poitevin allies. He would pay some compensation to Ralph for the loss of his Norman lands.

'I have money in strong chests stored with the Templars of La Rochelle; they will take care of it easily. And your mother, the Dowager Countess of Angoulême, we can pay her a final settlement I think. Some annual pension and some coin for now, immediately. I will write another letter to the master of the temple, he can release silver for her too.'

Alice de Courtenay, a granddaughter of a King of France, John's mother-in- law, another proud woman who had to bend her knee to him!

'You will increase her pension? So that you can continue to rule over my Angoulême? So that she cannot make any claim on Angoulême? You seem mightily concerned about Angoulême again.' Isabella read his face with bitterness. When would she have control of her inheritance?

'Too many questions, my queen. I need to see all my family gathered here, who knows how useful they can be? I am thinking marriage treaties, French dukes, Poitevin lords. Where might we negotiate? And Eleanor of Brittany could be someone's wife – I have always been good to her, she has eaten well in England and I have sent her robes and fine materials. But kept close, always kept close. It was good that I could marry off her half-sister Alix to one of my cousins. That makes Brittany safe for me.'

'But Eleanor, like me, is a true heir, she is the real heiress of Brittany, not some other. She has a good blood claim to that duchy. And you have kept her prisoner for a dozen years.' Isabella was spitting now. 'And you keep her under the custody of that Peter de Mauley, that wicked man, and now given Corfe Castle for his own. He is sent to buy the clothes for her, to take her these gifts. A man who helped you get rid of her brother.'

'Do not speak of such foul acts. You know nothing,

186

nothing – who tells you these lies? Now we are back near your home you seem very sure of yourself, madam.'

Isabella swung back at him. 'I am as sure of myself here as anywhere. I hope you notice me at your side. I am here where others are not.'

For Aimery de Thouars, that twister in the wind, turned against him once more just as John was poised to win, calling out to the assembled Poitevins and leading them away. They all withdrew and rode home to Parthenay, to Poitiers, to Niort, to Angoulême, to Lusignan. And John retreated and made for La Rochelle; he could not advance.

'A very shaming falling-back, I think.'

John paced the room, biting at his knuckles, turning every few steps, pent-up, furious, ready to explode. 'Be quiet, Isabella – hold that sharp tongue of yours before it cuts you. We are safe but need more knights, to help in the recovery of our territory. I will write to the earls and barons of England and all their lieges, I bear no one ill will even if they have not supported us so far. If they come now, we will be prosperous again. But I have strengthened Angoulême, the defences there are good. And I have told the knights at the castle in Ribérac to give it to a new constable, a powerful man who will guard that approach. He is trusted but I need to rally others – generally the Poitevins do not serve me well.'

Isabella began to speak, but he wheeled around to face her, glaring at her.

'Hah! You have served me, yes, that by the Mass I do say with some truth, you have served my purposes. Who else has served you, I wonder? Remember what I can do to any who think to swive with the queen. Or indeed what I can do to a queen who chooses to dally with some common man.'

Isabella quickly hung her head so he could not see her face, full of distress, and then just as quickly looked up, controlled and icy. She began to speak, and again he stopped her.

'And I must tell you that Oliver Bonneville died on the banks of the Loire. So many drowned as we came back from La Roche aux Moins, so much lost there. All the supplies, the tents and too many men. Perhaps you remember him? A knight from Angoulême, he had a brother, younger, who is in England, married to some country lady. That one had better come here and fight for me again.'

Isabella remembered and thought of Agnes, who had dallied there for a while before she had been left behind when John sailed so expediently and so secretly from France. Agnes had found a group of merchants known to her father, and they had escorted her home. Messages came from time to time and Isabella always hoped to see her again. She shook her head in weary disgust.

'Such a plight you find yourself in. Will you make friends with those who have so many grudges against you, and you against them? You sound confident, John, but I know you: your resolution, your will becomes a creeping thing, it fades away just at the moment when you should be going forward. Will you watch from a distance now as they fight further north?'

And Isabella left the room, her biting words hanging in the air.

The students danced in Paris for seven days, celebrating the French victory against both the English army and the armies of the princes from the Rhineland. A victory won on that hot and dusty late July day in the open field near Boulogne, a victory at Bouvines won in a melée and confusion, and the Capetians secure on their throne in Paris and all their possessions won from the English safely tucked under their flag. Normandy, Brittany, Anjou, Maine and Touraine; all lost because the Poitevin barons would not stay loyal to John. And the five-year truce signed with Philippe, and 60,000 marks paid by a king whose coffers were empty; who sulked in Aquitaine, where his pregnant wife did not bite her lip against the harsh words that were pent up inside her. Furious, passionate quarrels and furious, passionate reconciliations. It had been an unstable time for all.

They left France, and Joan was left behind, taken to Lusignan to be kept there until she could marry Hugh X; a quiet four-year-old who cried when she said goodbye to her mother and brother. The ships sailed from La Rochelle and landed at Dartmouth, travelling up to Exeter.

'One of my dowry cities,' murmured Isabella to herself as they clattered over the drawbridge into the castle. Weak October sunshine lit up the red stone gatehouse and almost immediately an armed escort arrived, led by a large, square, fair man with a look of Jutland about him.

'This is Terric, he will make sure you are safe on any journeys that are to be made. It may be that you should go to Berkhamsted. Terric is constable of that place.'

'Is it not also mine? Part of my promised dowry?'

'Promised to you, of course, yours of course – you may want to make a good tour and take a long view of the domain and make your plans. I am mindful that you need some place in court life, some further position. You have made this plain. We will stay in Exeter together for a few days and then I must ride on to Dorset and London. Terric will guard you, for I would have you guarded, my lady.'

'Indeed you would, for I am big with child.' She turned away, haughty, disdainful, only to be spun around. A twitching, black-gloved hand held her arm.

'Be very careful how you conduct yourself. Terric will see all and he will be just, he has been used to going between the several courts of Europe, and I trust him.

'I am with your child, our fourth child, do you think me a fool?

189

Terric was watchful and careful. He spoke little French but together they managed some English; straightforward, plain language. She regarded him as he gave commands, organised the packhorses and kept a hawk eye on the carts. He was useful; she could see that. He managed men and animals with a calm skill. Isabella liked him; it was good to relax into such care.

At the end of the month a messenger arrived from London with letters for the men waiting at Exeter and a letter for Terric. Nothing for her, but the letter commanded her to leave for Berkhamsted.

Take good care of the custody we have entrusted to you, letting us know regularly of the condition of this custody. Witnessed by myself (the king) at the Tower of London, 30th day of October.

And so they travelled up to Hertfordshire and its small wooded manors and gentle valley farms. Isabella was carried in a litter, no longer able to ride, watching the countryside unfold: Hampshire, and then the long, straight road to the town of Reading. The solid stone of Berkhamsted Castle, the gatehouse and the moat, a safe place and an important one. Mine, thought Isabella; mine – I was given this as part of my dowry and Terric has been made constable. We will be glad of this.

John arrived back in Corfe when the winter gales beat at the headland. He wrote to Terric: another journey was to be made, somewhere safer than Berkhamsted for the birth.

'Now, my lady queen, I think you must to Gloucester Castle for the birth. Your lying-in time is due, the Christmas feast is due but you are heavy with child and will be out of sight this year. The room where Joan was nursed would be a good place for this birth.'

'Am I being punished for my plain speaking? Well, Terric, my lord the king orders us to go to Gloucester. I would wish him Godspeed but my heart shuts my mouth.'

But for John there was too much trouble elsewhere to be dealing with a fretful, pregnant wife. He simply wrote to Terric to be vigilant, and keep his charges carefully.

XVII

England, 1215

The early part of the New Year was as cold as it could be, as cold as a whetstone, but by February Isabella was moving again, following her restless husband, with Terric at her side, Henry and Richard riding with her and baby Isabelle cradled with her nursemaid, all making for Marlborough and the Nevilles. Marlborough was busy, with the scribes writing charters, Terric called to be a witness for one, and the treasury in the castle paying out thousands of marks. Hugh de Neville kept the keys, holding onto this safe haven, this stronghold. It was more than just a place for good hunting now.

'He expects mercenaries from France, from Gascony and the Poitevin,' Terric told Isabella. 'And many castles are being repaired. Garrisons strengthened, too. There is trouble north of here. And in London. The barons meet, grumble. Those northerners want to settle grievances this year. Old grievances rub hard.

'If he goes north, he will hunt – he likes the hunting with his hawks. It is good up there for sport.'

A listless reply. Isabella was tired: being pregnant again so soon after Isabelle's birth was a wearisome business. She thought it would be peaceful to be somewhere without all this bustle and dealing with messengers and summonses, somewhere that was more her own. She found John before he rode out – he was as impatient as always, but for once, not angry and challenging with her. They stood together, and he reached out a hand to cup her belly.

'Another baby? We were fierce together the last time, my lady.'

'Yes, another baby, and my churching for Isabelle just two weeks past. It will be born when the harvest comes in – I feel heavy already and need some restful place. I would go to Berkhamsted for that.'

'Then go there – Terric is your knight and will guard you well. He tells me you need two more carthorses for the baggage. It will be arranged and I will send wine for the cellar and wax for the candles. Everything you need or want.' He pulled her to him and briefly she rested her head on his shoulder. Then they both stood back and regarded each other gravely.

'Keep the children safe.'

'Always, my lord.'

Berkhamsted was tranquil in the thin, late winter sunshine and Isabella took comfort in the slow walks around the keep, early violets spangling the grass. A few weeks of almost solitude, and then came reports that the king was at Oxford, but that she must move back to Marlborough.

The castle was heaving with knights arrived from the West Country, and the Nevilles were preoccupied. A constant stream of deliveries to be attended to: arms, crossbows, bolts, armour.

Joan Neville took a few minutes to sit with Isabella, and warned her that trouble was coming.

'The barons and Archbishop Langton are intent on restoring ancient laws, ancient customs. They have written out a list to present to the king. Contrary to reason they make these demands.'

'And the king, he refuses? I would not expect anything else – such a list will be greeted with his fury.'

'Indeed it has been, and so the barons say they will seize his castles and lands. They have found a leader, Fitzwalter, whom they call Marshal of the Army of God and Holy Church.'

Isabella listened but fretted; supplies were needed for her small group. More almonds for almond milk – the least she wanted; no one could consider her table extravagant. John sent instructions for her to be supplied with sacks of almonds, and fish for Friday and Saturday meals: small pike and some roach. Always making sure of the details, Isabella thought, as she ordered them to be cooked with parsley and garlic and served with carrots, a modest way of filling the plates. And he sent silk to her, a length of soft aquamarine blue that she could make into an underskirt to cover her swelling belly. She stroked the material and thought of the new baby; already fluttering and turning, a good, strong quickening.

And then John himself arrived, riding fast up from Corfe, furious with the barons. He railed at the rebellion, scornful and fierce. The king's royal anger, his dark displeasure could send even his friends into disgrace, but now there were men who openly rebelled. Who would be enemies.

'I would fine them if I could, several hundred marks. Take their lands and castles. They are suspicious at all times, very suspicious, and they want everything. Making great trouble with these unjust demands, with their great list! A schedule – a list so long, and they seek such things which are made up, invented with no reason. Nothing is believable – their brains are full of whey and curds. By the feet of God, I wonder that they don't they ask for the kingdom itself!'

Savage words were shouted that caused fear and loathing. John had become less and less tolerant, if that was possible, his rages and anger bewildering the maids and children, who watched at a distance a father who bit his knuckles or chewed up sticks like an angry dog, punched the walls, yelling at their mother or cuffing a servant.

'Hush, he is angry not with you: the wars in France did not go well and we have many possessions lost to us. And now there are wars here with the barons.'

'He has said that I must go to Corfe Castle, to live there.' Richard stood in front of Isabella, determined to be strong and brave.

'And so you will, with your tutor and two men to accompany you and tell all how important you are. They will use their trumpets and make a great noise for Richard of Cornwall!'

And then John was gone, still angry with the barons, fuming about how they would try to make him seal a charter of liberties.

Terric brought news from her half-brother, asking for permission to come to England. King Philippe had been asked for a licence and safe conduct was wanted.

'What is this? Why does Peter de Joigny come now? Is he concerned about the state of England, Terric?'

'To offer you protection, I would believe. Shelter from the trouble. He is unsure of who is to be trusted at this time. Some are, some are not, and who can say where the trust falls?'

'I say no one can be trusted. John advances one, like Hugh de Neville, a man he is happy to have by his side, to gamble the night away with. The chief forester, and so very powerful. And yet his wife Joan must escape from the lechery of a king. If you can escape from the king's ill will, his violent ill will, and have not lost then there is no danger. I have tried to keep safe from that. To keep out of danger.'

Terric agreed that it was important, and that she was adept at making sure of her safety. Isabella continued.

'Peter may be ruined by John: the king is often heavy-

195

handed, capricious. He makes sour comments about our family friendship. But let him come – I would not tell him do not come, even if the times are turbulent.'

The barons had marched to Northampton. They tried to take the castle, but after two weeks it was still with the king.

'Futile attempt, no siege engines. Their standard bearer died, along with many others. Pierced through the head by a crossbow bolt. It is good we have those crossbows and their bolts. And the king writes here of our barons who are against us. Pah! Our barons, as he calls them, will soon be known as the enemies they are.'

'Am I safe here? And the children, I must keep them safe.'

'For now, yes – this place is to have its defences shored up. I am commanded to Winchester to help oversee some more fortification there. The king has written to all his castles to resist attack, from Newark to Launceston. A great sweep of the land.'

'Is Winchester not safe anymore? Henry is at Winchester. What of the bishop? Des Roches is so strong I thought he could ward off any army!' A quick decision as Isabella took in the news. 'I will come with you to Winchester. I want to see Henry again, perhaps he should come back here to be with me. The king will allow that: his heir should be with me, in case…' Her voice trailed away; she did not dare say what she thought.

So Henry rode back to Marlborough with Isabella, and seemed pleased to be with his mother and baby sister.

More news; Joan Neville hurried in with an anxious face. London had opened its gates to the rebel army.

'The king gave them a charter! The right to an annual election of all future mayors, and all their liberties that they have had before, all that they were granted to use, confirmed! A good charter, a generous charter. You would think the city would support the king after such a gift! But no, they open up the gates.'

'Not a gift,' said Isabella, 'not a gift at all. A bribe, except the bribe was not enough because they hate him too much.'

Joan was almost talking to herself, worrying away at the problems of sedition. 'It is a very bad thing to have the capital in rebel hands. The Treasury is there, and the Exchequer – it is a most parlous state for the king. London is so rich. And listen, Isabella: not only all that loss, but the palace at Westminster, and the abbey. Dreadful news.'

'The abbey is where all of the kings of England have their coronation, is it not? Perhaps one day, Henry...' Isabella broke off. Why where her thoughts running on Henry's succession all the time? She turned to Joan and smiled. 'And someone could just sail up the Thames and claim the throne and be crowned in that abbey. I wonder who could do such a thing? Someone French, perhaps? I would expect no less from Philippe and his son: they are intent on England again. Normandy is theirs, why not London too? But we have Henry safe here. The next coronation will be his, not Louis'.'

Isabella walked away, her mind teeming with the possibilities that were beginning to group and regroup.

'Hush, hush, to speak like that! The king will order reprisals, you see, against these false men of London, and you must not speak as if you approve of their way. It is fraud and treason.' Joan frowned after Isabella. This wife, this queen was sometimes very sharp, and her language disloyal.

Terric came back from Winchester. John had been there getting pledges for defences, ordering timber to bolster the castle and judging whether this ancient seat of English kings could be used again, if London was lost.

'The Welsh and the Scots are making trouble too. The king will need to confer with these barons.'

197

'Is he still bringing men from Poitou and Gascony to fight for him here? Yes? I thought as much. Foreign knights and bowmen, all to garrison his castles – no wonder the barons do not trust him! These men will be paid in confiscated lands – John will enjoy taking their estates and giving them to his men from the Aquitaine.'

'War exists, my lady – this is what happens in war. He has asked them to think again. To take back their oath against him. To be reconciled. And if they did that, well he would see that they made no offence. Against their king.

'A long proposal of peace that, Terric!'

Terric was not listening, working out what could happen, what risks there might be for the queen and her children.

'Something is needed now that London has fallen. As I said, there will need to be some talks, some discussion between John and these barons. They are so full of themselves now, turning down offer after offer. And John dare not go further than Windsor. They have seized London, what if they come on and on?'

At the end of May, men arrived, carthorses carrying chests with all the jewels, the regalia that had belonged to Matilda, locked away for safety. The magnificent collection that once Isabella had unwrapped and then packed again, lingering over the wealth and beauty, a true celebration of an empress and her power. To be kept here for a while, but John would want it with him, of that she was sure.

In early June, Terric brought more news. He was riding out every day and meeting the mercenaries; he knew some of the guard from Flanders and they were full of the story.

'It is done: there was a meeting in a water meadow by the Thames, the barons on one bank and the king on the other. Tents, pavilions and flags flying – the three lions for the king, and the barons showing their allegiances with their banners. They marched out from London and crossed the old bridge at Staines to reach him. John had offered safe conduct to all who would cross to Runnymede.'

'What happened next? Did he rail at them, his barons, his enemies? Did he want peace?'

'He ordered his most loyal commanders to keep the truce, and indeed he extended the truce past the day set. He was intent on reconciliation.'

'Reconciliation is not a word I have heard that often when my husband is negotiating. And the rebel barons, how furious they are with him: the tyranny that is his reign, indeed his way of being. And then there is the loss of lands in France. They have turned on him once and they will do so again.'

'The charter, the Articles of the Barons, is sealed: all demands discussed, all terms revised. A basis for peace. And to witness the issue, twenty-five in all, to enforce the charter.'

'Who, who? Tell me some names.'

'Des Roches, of course, and Hugh Neville, de Burgh, Geoffrey Fitzpeter and William, Earl of Salisbury.'

'The earl, whom John would try to cuckold while he was out of England and imprisoned in France last autumn! A most forgiving knight.'

'And it is good that men from all parts of France were present, the Touraine and Poitou, to witness the issue. Some so anxious to prevent a war, all counselling him.'

'I would say that some of these counsellors are evil.' Isabella looked hard at Terric. She was thinking of Peter des Roches, from the Touraine, unpopular and oppressive to all.

'But none of the rebels witnessed the charter, for they have foresworn their fealty. When we have peace they will make their homage. For now they stand by.'

'I wish that all remain loyal, but I have seen what happens in France. Those that swear fealty serve him well while there are rewards, but can turn elsewhere when more is offered.

I have been offered plenty but given nothing.' And Isabella turned away and walked into her chamber. She wanted to hear no more.

A firm peace has been made between us and the barons and the freemen of our kingdom, John wrote. For indeed they had made him seal the charter, those advisers and witnesses, the Charter of Runnymede, a charter John then laughed to scorn. The charter that said a king who claimed to be chosen by God was not above the law. Stephen Langton, so stern and unyielding, standing over John, who had sniggered up his sleeve within weeks. And the rebel barons were not to be rebuked and disobeyed; they took their revenge in declaring for war, and for Prince Louis to come from France and be their king.

John worked his way through Dover, Rochester and Canterbury. He had been purposeful, intent and determined; ordering pickaxes, burning and looting and marauding through the towns. He had showed his contempt for God by stabling horses in a cathedral. John detested Langton, the cleric forced upon him.

'They will not last as men of so-called courage and reso-lution, these barons – I have set fear in them. You wait and see! Already many are proving to be nothing but drunken sots, cowards as well as traitors. Well, let them carouse, I am taking no prisoners in this war.'

The French had marched on London, called by the English barons to take the crown and throne of England. They would rather have Prince Louis, Philippe's son, than John. If the bar-ons could use Louis to unseat this tyrant then they would. And Louis's wife had a strong strength of purpose. Blanche, daughter of Eleanor of Castile, granddaughter of Henry II and brought by her grandmother, Queen Eleanor, across the Pyrenees all those years ago to be married to Louis in Normandy.

It was Blanche who gave Louis the right to be considered King of England. A pair of holy mice, Isabella had thought, but Blanche was strong and forceful. A great deal of her grandmother seemed to live on in her. She had been the one who mustered the French ships to cross the Channel and invade; an invasion that had quickly conquered the south and taken London.

Isabella held tight to Henry's hand. He had just turned eight and would be king eventually, and who knew what that would bring for her as the mother of a king? And now, while the battles were fought at a great distance from the safety of the west, she could plan a future; think about being regent. Perhaps she could be part of a negotiation with Louis? She could try to work something to the advantage of England, of her son. She wished that they would let her talk to the French, as much as she disliked Louis and Blanche with their clever, quick, eager ambitions. John was so disliked it would be difficult to rescue him from any of the French designs, but a regency, with Isabella as a pivotal player? Surely something such as this could come about? But not while she was mewed up in this castle, gleaning scraps of news.

John had been harrying the north, scouring the place, knocking out resistance, and now he was making his way to Lincoln. There was a possibility he would go to Lynn. It was useless to think about where he might be; messengers and news were muddled.

Isabella worried that she could not ride out for herself but here she was, and here she had to stay, kept safe by Terric and his men. She had no great court around her, only a dozen servants and a wet nurse.

XVIII

Bristol Castle, Gloucester Castle,
Gloucester Abbey, Corfe Castle England, 1216

And now John was dead. He was dead, and the French invasion must surely come to an end.

The messenger was still fumbling with the leather pouch that contained all the official notes and seals, sent by William Marshall. Isabella pulled her wandering thoughts and wits together. She had better find out more about her husband's death; she would have to tell the children and by God's teeth, her son was now king.

'Tell me what happened. I know the army was to the east and working north again.'

'There was a need to reach Wisbech Castle, from Lynn. The king was ill with a fever and belly cramps – he wanted to stay there to rest for he had been riding forty miles a day. Such hot haste for all his men and horses. So he crossed the Wellstream where it runs into the estuary, but he sent the baggage train separately, full of goods, linen, wool cloth, his wardrobe, some provisions and armour…all sent across the estuary called the Reaping or Cutting-Off Estuary. And the treasure too, my lady.' This last was said with a low, hasty voice and a glance at the woman standing by the window, one hand on the wall as she listened with a bowed head.

'The treasure?'

'Yes, the king's own jewels and the crowns of England.'

Not only of England: there were Matilda's crowns, brought from Germany. Isabella groaned. She knew them so well, had recorded their intricate details, so beautiful and so valuable, laden with precious stones.

'Go on.'

'It was a disaster, the crossing was a disaster: there were mudflats and marshes and you can traverse these at low tide, but they are dangerous to the unwary, riddled with quicksand and deeper channels. Vulnerable to a surging tide.'

'Why did the king choose such a dangerous route? Why in God's name take a path across with heavy carts?'

'There is a causeway and ford across the mouth of the Wellstream. This can be used when the tide is low. And if you pay for local guides, they will take you the safest way.'

'And John was paying them? His knights paid for guides? No, I thought not. Fools! It would have been vital to know the way or be in danger from the sea.'

'And the sea was rising – the horse-drawn wagons moved too slowly for the incoming tide, and many were lost. Perhaps some wagons were caught and this blocked the others, leaving them to the mercy of the rush of water. Overturned and swept away, sunk. Rising waters, quicksand...'

'How many crossed?'

'Perhaps two thousand soldiers and servants. It saved them some nine miles and the king's mood was so angry they wished to press on, they were in a hurry to meet him on the road.'

'Too many to cross quickly at any time. And then what happened? John had no men, no servants, no baggage train? Only the royal party?'

'He stayed at Wisbech Castle for one night and then rode to near Boston, to the abbey at Swineshead. It is a well-endowed abbey: there is a good farm there and the monks from the Cistercian order are strong workers. They were sympathetic to the tremendous ill fortune of the king and fed him well with the harvest festival fruits: pears, peaches and new cider.'

'Still feverish and cramping and he eats raw fruit and drinks cider!'

'Yes, my lady. He was very thirsty and the cider refreshed him, but his body was weakening and the bloody flux was seen in his stools.'

'Weak and ill, all precious treasure lost, men lost – only the king's party to ride with him, but to where?'

'To Sleaford first and then he struggled on to Newark, to the Bishop of Lincoln's castle. He had to be carried in a litter the men made for him, panting and groaning all the way. He cried out in pain and rage – the road was rough and difficult. It was piteous. But then he managed to ride again, on a slow, old horse, to the castle. He collapsed and lay there for two days, but even though they brought in the abbot of Croxton, a man with medical skill, he was so ill he could not read the letters sent to him, or write to you. And so the abbot confessed him and gave him the viaticum, the final communion. That night a dreadful storm howled all around.'

Isabella thought of John being absolved of all sins, his body anointed with holy oil as it had been when he was crowned, a crucifix held for him to gaze upon so that he should meditate on the Redeemer. She felt anger and tears tightening her throat; longed to shout to the world that it was an ambitious, impatient tyrant who had died, not some great king; he had been corrupted by power and she along with him, by him.

'His body goes where? It was embalmed?'

'Yes, and the abbot took away his heart and his guts and sent a monk to mount vigil over the body and say Mass for his soul.'

'For his soul,' she repeated and thought of the French prophecy: John shall die a landless king, in a litter. Well, he had escaped that, but only just, and would he now escape Hell? 'His mortal body could go to the monks at Beaulieu, for he founded that place.'

The abbey he had founded for the love of God, for the souls of Henry his father, Richard, Eleanor and all his ancestors and heirs. No mention of Isabella. Her face darkened: he had never asked for prayers for her, or mentioned her when dedicating charters.

'He asked for his body to be buried at Worcester Priory – his armed mercenaries have already conducted it there. They were Poitevin men, I believe.'

Isabella made a small surprised sound. She had not realised there were still such men in John's retinue, but it was good to think of him, the most treacherous of kings, being taken to his final resting place by the most disloyal of all. She considered the route.

'Yes, that was right and proper, a safer journey than to ride across to us here in the west.'

But now she must summon the children and tell them that their father was dead, and plan how to make sure that Henry was crowned without delay. Westminster was out of the question; London still held by the rebels: they would have to use Gloucester Cathedral. And was there news of any regency? Who was to help her son begin his reign? A queen mother was important and useful to a young boy. She would need to write letters to all those who might support her. Isabella turned to the exhausted messenger slumped against the door.

'Go to the kitchens and find some hot food. Your horse has been stabled? Good. Your news is unhappy but the future holds good.'

The messenger handed over the leather bag and left, glad

not to have been asked about the king's household after John died, more plundering than mourning. He had been glad, too, of the commission to ride to tell the news to the queen, away from the fighting and with sixpence in his pocket.

Isabella carried the pouch to her chamber to see what messages had been sent to her along with the seals. There were none, just a note confirming John's death, and that more news would come as soon as possible.

Peter des Roches arrived the next day. Peter des Roches, Bishop of Winchester that clever man brought over from France by John, and so favoured by him. A foreigner like her, and suddenly Isabella felt very alien standing there; waiting to be told what was going to happen next. She needed to get her words in first because he and William Marshall would take absolute charge if she did not make her mark at once.

She had the children around her: Henry pale, with his one eye drooping, the one mark he had inherited from John. But he stood still and with a grave air. Now he knew he was king he was fearful of what was expected of him: would he have to fight the French? Richard stood with his hands on his hips, his truculent lower lip pushed out; the two youngest girls holding hands with the nursemaid and ready to cry if you so much looked at them. And Joan was away in Lusignan, six years old and making the long preparation to become the countess, to marry Hugh le Brun, the son of the man whom Isabella had once been so proud to be betrothed to. Isabella had scarcely given her a thought in all this: Joan was out of the civil war in England, safe in the Poitevin, not to be worried about when there were far more important and pressing matters.

Peter knelt in front of Henry, his right hand on his heart, head bowed. 'Your Majesty.'

Isabella gently pushed Henry and he stepped forward to be clasped in an embrace. He looked up at Peter des Roches who had taught him to read, arranged for him to learn to ride, scolded his table manners, and now this man knelt to him. Isabella swept forward and was kissed on both cheeks by Peter des Roches, who whispered in her ear, 'I have some news for you of an inheritance.' And then so the boys could hear, 'The funeral of your father, the king was a true service, he was buried in royal robes and silks draped over his tomb. And William Marshall was there to make sure all was well and indeed he mourned him deeply. '

'No crown,' Isabella spoke bitterly, 'no crown, lost to England, that royal crown.'

'And tomorrow we must ride to meet Marshall; he has sent an escort for Henry and his family. The Queen Dowager and her two sons, for would you bring Richard of Cornwall too? But leave the infant daughters behind, young for this journey and safer here.'

Already I am being ordered about as if I had no say in any of this, they have made their plans and now I must obey. Isabella's face was cold and calm but she seethed inside as she made her small household ready. She shook out her new fur lined cloak, the last present from John, sent to her after Eleanor's birth, a daughter he had never seen. Then she carefully packed her Queen's seal and jewellery into the small, iron and leather bound chest that went with her everywhere.

The roads were wet and muddy with trees down because a week of gales had swept across the west of England. They were riding to Malmsebury, a town about thirty miles away, built on a steep hill and almost surrounded by rivers. There was an abbey there where they could shelter for the night for it would be a hard day's ride.

Isabella rode behind Peter des Roches in sour silence, Terric rode with Henry and Richard, encouraging them as they grew tired. All were determined to make Malmsebury before night fall.

And there in the road, as they finally approached the hill

that led up to the town, was William Marshall, grey and grizzled. He had achieved his three score years and ten but was still strong and upright as he stood by his horse.

Terric lifted Henry from his pony and carried him towards Marshall who wept when he saw the small boy in the arms of the tall solid knight. Henry was crying too as he looked at this old man who had known his grandfather, his uncle and his father, the best knight of all who looked after England, his tutor had told him. Would he look after Henry? He hoped so.

'I give myself over to God and to you, so that in the Lord's name you may take charge of me.'

'I will be yours in good faith. There is nothing I will not do to serve you while I have the strength.'

The next morning they all made the cavalcade to Gloucester. 'Indeed, he is worth fighting for.' Isabella was walking about the great hall of Gloucester Castle, stamping her feet for emphasis as she faced Peter des Roches and William Marshall. 'Am I to see what John has decided for our son, because it seems to me that as the queen mother I should be at my son's side at this difficult time. I would speak with Louis and tell him to leave our country. We can declare a charter or manifesto in Henry's name that would pull all those rebels back to allegiance.'

Peter and William exchanged glances and then Peter unfolded the brief will that John had dictated as he lay dying. Isabella seized it and read.

Being overtaken by a grievous sickness, and so incapable of making a detailed disposition of my goods...faithful men whose names I have written below...ordainers and executors of my will Gualo, legate of the Apostolic See, Peter, lord Bishop of Winchester, Richard, lord Bishop of Chichester, Silvester, lord Bishop of Worcester, William Marshall, Earl of Pembroke, Ranulf, Earl of Chester, Walter Lacy, John of Monmouth, Fawkes de Breauté...

'And so on, and so on, thirteen names in all, but no words written of my Queen Isabella, who shall be regent!'

'No, you are not named in his will in this regard. You are to be gifted a sum of money, 3,500 marks – that is his special mention for your continued health and prosperity.'

'My continued prosperity! You well know I have nothing of my own. I have safeguarded the succession by bearing two sons, I have had three daughters who can be married to strengthen ties, and all my children live. A steady succession of children, and my health is good as you can see. I am of strong stock. But I have had no court of my own, and my patronage, which I desired to use wisely, was not possible with no possession of my dower, no queen's gold. And now no regency.'

Peter des Roches put out an arm, and spoke soothingly. 'It is a difficult time for us all. You must know that there have been rumours of gross adultery, that you are said to be a depraved woman, and this perhaps influenced the king.'

'Adultery! The king was as unfaithful as a cock on the dung heap, he enjoyed many a high-born lady in his bed and everyone knows that. He made free with the wives and daughters of his barons, his lustful ways were legion. The worst story of all was that of Matilda Fitzwalter, the Fair Matilda. He wanted her so badly, ignoring me, sending me away again. He stalked the Fitzwalter family, he imprisoned Matilda in the turret of White Tower in London, where she died. Stories came, foul stories about an egg, boiled up with poison, given to her to eat when she refused John yet again. And you say that I am depraved! I have been sent from castle to castle with the children, and our youngest born last year. He ensured that I was well employed in being pregnant and out of the way.' Isabella stood square, facing them, daring them to continue.

'There was talk of a young knight, enjoyed by yourself

in the high summer of a few years back, and found hanged, strangled, dangling at the head of your bed, the cords of the curtains knotted about his neck. It was a warning about your fidelity…and then there was the matter of your half-brother, Peter de Courtney.'

The slap hit hard and Isabella raised her hand again, but William caught it.

'Hush, hush, this is no way to behave before the coronation. No doubt rumours, but we cannot have a queen mother tarred like this. We know that you were kept guarded more than once, and that you were to be kept close most carefully, for more reasons than safety. So for now we will all be quiet and pray for peace in our realm with the new king.'

'I have been written about in the most slanderous of ways, and will not listen to your stories. No one should believe them – so many lies! Once they said I had been raped and Henry murdered, or Richard murdered, and that was an untruth as you well know, as is all the rest of the scurrilous gossip. I am no sorceress, do not be anxious about me in that regard.'

And she left the hall, head held high, and her way so haughty and proud that the guards on the door wondered to kneel as she passed though.

Almost the end of October, ten days after his father's death, Henry stood quiet in the abbey church in Gloucester, while the papal legate Gualo bustled around directing the bishops and congregated barons. The royal regalia lost, and they were far from Westminster. And the Archbishop of Canterbury, Stephen Langton, was supporting Louis – not a churchman that anyone this day wished to see near the new young king.

Royal robes had been hastily cut down to fit Henry; he had been knighted by William Marshall for only a dubbed knight could become a king. But there was one more problem to consider: what would they use to crown the boy?

'I have a corolla made of gold, it has been mine since my wedding day. I think it will fit my son's head.'

Isabella took the beaten gold circle out of the small chest and polished it carefully with a silk rag. She had tried to find out who Gualo thought should be regent, but been brushed aside. Now she must play at being the diplomat and try to guide events as much as possible.

'England's treasure is lost, Henry. Your father lost it in his furious journey across the estuary, the estuary that cuts off the land so fiercely that it mows down baggage carts as if they were ninepins. So there is no crown for you. But you can wear this and be proud, for your father gave it to me when we were married.'

Peter des Roches took it from her, and he and Gualo blessed the simple gold band.

Silvester, the Bishop of Worcester and Simon, the Bishop of Exeter processed with Henry to the altar where they anointed him. Peter des Roches placed the small crown on his head and the loyalist barons cheered. A boy king was a problem, but this one was a fair young knight and not tainted with his father's character. It would be better to have him on the throne in England than Prince Louis. There was still something to fight for.

The barons met again and talk rumbled around the great castle hall, everyone pleased to have seen yesterday's coronation.

'A very moving ceremony, good to see a young knight stand so straight, become a king before us all. We will remember this day.'

'William Marshall is still loyal to the cause, and with enough men to support the war in some significance.'

'And what of the queen? She stands close to her son, and

there is the other boy, Richard of Cornwall. A lioness with two cubs – she could be formidable.'

'No experience. Ambitious, I understand, and looking to be the regent, but what influence has she had in politics at court? Her sway was in the bedchamber and that place is cold now. Her reason for marrying John was all ambition, she was dazzled by the crown.'

'What do you think of the Earl of Chester? He has been ever loyal too.'

'And powerful, most powerful. Would he want the regency? When does he arrive here?'

And so they talked and listened, and Gualo wove between the fighting men, assessing the mood and making decisions. Ranulf, the Earl of Chester was a consideration, a last survivor of the great feudal aristocracy. If given lucrative favours, his fidelity would stay firm.

Events were moving quickly, too quickly for Isabella to influence the outcome. She watched from the gallery, her face blank, but inside she seethed. Without a doubt most wanted William Marshall to be chosen: elderly he might be, but such a figurehead. She had no presence among this gathering. She had been discounted. Marshall was put forward and offered the regency by the nobles and the clerics.

'I will wait until the Earl of Chester joins us and then we can discuss again.' A diplomatic response from that able tactician.

There was a concerned grumble: would Ranulf object? Would there be conflict here where none was wanted by any?

A stirring as Ranulf arrived and pushed into the room. A quick conference, and then he shook his head. 'I have no wish to be regent, and indeed I would ask William Marshall to be that necessary man.'

Gualo added his request again, the bishops nodding assent.

William leant back against the high, rough stone wall and

spoke to the company. 'I am standing here with my back to the wall – indeed, it might be considered a symbol of the position we now find ourselves in, but I will be the regent for Henry III. Long live the king!'

Cheers from all, and eager movements.

'And while I can, I will carry him from land to land on my shoulders if need be, one leg here and one leg there. Ireland is safe and the regency court and government could make its way to Dublin.'

But this was argued not to be necessary; a place of safety would be found in England.

Isabella swore and raged in her room, as maids packed the chests for they would move back to Corfe or Marlborough or Winchester, not stay here. Henry was to go with Peter des Roches; he had said goodbye to his mother and brother and ridden away that morning. Isabella promised to follow when she could, taking his hand and explaining.

'There is little animosity towards you, Henry, but let us see who will declare for you this winter. I am determined that Louis will not have the throne, and surely those who thought to rebel will now turn away to the rightful king.'

She curtseyed to him, and Richard knelt briefly, a little scowl crossing his face as he stood. He hoped his brother would soon send for him: it was very boring being the only boy at Corfe. Isabella was full of hard, bitter thoughts.

'Marshall has swiftly taken command – he will be the regent and go off and lead the war effort, while Peter des Roches has been made Henry's guardian. I am to sit in the background again and be nothing.'

Peter des Roches, Gualo and William, a powerful triumvirate, agreed that the situation was grim, but also hoped that John's death would help the English crown. They also agreed that she, Isabella, was too much associated with the old regime, with controversy, scandal and gossip, to be offered any role on the council.

'This is a volatile time and the last thing we want is such a volatile woman – she struggles all the time to be considered as an influence. She is not to be thought of as a suitable counsellor. A sparkling beauty once and still to be admired, but sharp-tongued, very sharp-tongued.'

'There is no doubt in my mind that her marriage to John was a disaster for England. The king began the loss of Normandy within two years of the marriage, and England lost land and rich, rich revenues. We need to send new, clear messages about the government to the people, and she can be no part of those.'

Gualo swept into the scriptorium, his red cardinal robes flowing on the white stone floor, full of energy, committed to saving England. 'We are determined, and it has been decided by the regent, the Bishop of Winchester and myself that we need to make the Magna Carta survive. We will issue it again under the name of Henry III.'

'He has no seal to impress on it,' murmured one of the monks.

'Indeed, no – not yet, not yet, so my seal and the regent's seal will have to be used. Set to, set to.'

Come All Saint's Day, an early, chilly mist lay across Studland Bay, and Isabella, wrapped in her warm winter cloak, was working out what to do next. To secure her possessions was paramount and if she could not establish a position of influence within her son's fledgling court, then she would make sure of something tangible.

'Well, if I am to be ostracised I can at least have some say about my properties and what dower I can take.'

Isabella's clerks wrote to the sheriff of Devon, instructing him that:

214

Immediately and without delay the city of Exeter, and various other properties in Devon which have been assigned to me in my dower, should be handed over to me. My possession of the stannaries is of utmost urgency and importance.

She stamped the letter with her great seal, and there she is standing, facing front, robed and crowned, her hair falling in ringlets around her face. In her right hand she holds a flower, in her left a bird. Isabella, by the grace of God, Queen of England, Lady of Ireland. Isabella, Duchess of the Normans, of the Men of Aquitaine and of Anjou.

Isabella thought, I have lost all those dower lands in Normandy and Anjou; my position here in England is being frustrated at every turn. But my place in Aquitaine, my Angoulême inheritance, waits for me and to return home at this time when I am being turned aside, unheeded by these powerful men who do not appreciate my worth – that is a decision to rejoice in.

XIX

1217 England: Lincoln, Dover, London and Exeter
France: La Rochelle and Angoulême

April had been cold and wet with high spring tides, but at the end of the month Prince Louis had sailed back to England with new soldiers, intent on two things: besieging Lincoln and capturing Dover. When the May trees were showing white and green, that cunning old soldier William Marshall gambled on defeating the forces in a single battle. He mustered at Newark and made a fast march north, up Ermine Street to Lincoln, a crafty entry through a side gate and a fierce attack on the French knights and the belligerent band of rebels who surrounded the castle. The town was in French hands, but the castle, high on the hill, its foundations built over an old Roman fort; there the garrison held strong and all were for King Henry. The streets became the battleground as fierce fighting spilled into the centre. Marshall took the city and the castle.

'We secured the north gate and our crossbowmen were up on the rooftops – you can imagine what happened when so many volleys of bolts rained down from on high. Great confusion, much damage to soldiers, and if a man received a bolt his death was rapid. If we caught them in the street we cut them down like pigs. But that was not all: we needed to make a great charge against the French besiegers. We offered their leader surrender, but he chose to fight.'

The last was said with some admiration as William told the account to Henry. Peter des Roches kept silent. He had been there too, leading a division, but now he must listen. They were sitting in the hall at Winchester, a fire burning in the hearth and candles already lit.

'What happened then?' Henry was leaning forward; this was a tale worth telling, listening to and remembering. He would tell Richard about such a great battle; they could re-enact it and learn something.

'We won, it was a rout.' William took a great gulp of wine mixed with water.

'And their leader was killed?' Henry wanted it all tidied up and finished neatly.

'Yes, and we took many prisoners of note – good ransom money will follow. Some escaped and fled south to London, but rest assured, Your Majesty, it was a decisive victory, all over in six hours. Lady Nichola de Haye, the castellan, sends loyal greetings. She remembers your father well: she once offered the keys of the castle to him, saying she was too old and fatigued to guard the place any longer. He called her "beloved" and willed that she should keep the castle until he ordered otherwise, and so she has, and keeps it still for you, Majesty.'

And Marshall took his leave, feeling proud of his army, but weary.

Spring turned to high summer and the French fleet appeared of the coast of Kent: ships full of men, supplies and siege engines; a fleet raised by Blanche of Castile, an energetic, supportive wife. The French flagship was full of horses, treasure, men and a great trebuchet, causing the ship to be low in the water, overloaded and top-heavy.

Hubert de Burgh told the story, a forceful account that

young Henry appreciated. He had watched some of the action from the shore with William Marshall, but this was more exciting, this was a blow by blow description.

'We not only scattered them, we blew powdered lime in their faces – blinded 'em, and best of all, we captured this monk who turned pirate. Eustace – he was in the service of your father, had thirty ships from King John and went raiding against the French out of Sark. We needed him once upon a time but he switched sides, and he's been ferrying the French and Prince Louis across the Channel.'

The boy king listened intently; this was war as he had never expected it to be.

'We found him hiding in the bilges. Oh, he offered huge sums of money for his life: 10,000 marks, a good price for a ransom and the money useful, but the crews hated him, so we cut off his head!'

Roars of laughter and approval.

The autumn saw a flurry of meetings: Lambeth, Kingston, Staines, Merton, each meeting with a treaty to sign. The regents signed at Lambeth, others at Kingston, Gualo giving papal ratification and making known a few terms of his own.

Isabella sneered when she saw Louis in Kingston. The court was Chertsey, and so far she was clinging onto being part of the court, if not the council. 'You come to the table – you are forced to the table, to sue for peace. No English crown for you and your clever wife.'

Louis smiled thinly. Des Roches and William Marshall gestured her to be quiet, to stop pushing her way into the debate.

'We are offering an amnesty to rebels. Prince Louis and his supporters will not be excommunicated, but must do penance.'

'And what of territory? He has no claim to the throne of England and will make none ever again, not for himself or through his wife? He will admit that he was never a legitimate

King of England?' Isabella was not to be silenced. This could be her only chance to speak for her son; she would have him King of England and it would be a peaceful kingdom.

'Prince Louis will give up all claims, will not attack again and for that we give him 10,000 marks, a sum which offers some consolation.'

Isabella was not finished. 'And the Channel Islands? Used by that pirate monk as safe harbours, places to hide ships, and they proved strong bases for him. The king saw them as important: they were part of Normandy but not lost with Normandy. They must remain with the crown.'

'No doubt they will be useful to the crown at times.' Marshall wished that she would stop forcing issues onto the table. He wanted Louis to leave London, to go back to France and his wife, placated. Marshall needed to set about restoring order now that John was dead and he was regent.

'They refuse to give me any role!' Isabella fumed and fretted, and thought again of the choices that could be made. Henry was living in the household of Peter des Roches and taken up with all the skills necessary for full knighthood and war. Eleanor and Isabelle, only two and three years old, had joined him there, along with Henry's nursemaid whom he loved dearly.

More than me. Isabella's thoughts were sour. And they will need a long time to make Henry a warrior: he likes to study and is full of piety, most unlike his father, poring over the scriptures and stories of the saints. And Richard is at Corfe Castle with de Mauley, that wily Poitevin – Richard will be well served there, close enough to the West Country which is to be his domain when he is older. He is like his grandfather, I think, strong and forceful.

There were loud whispers now, telling the story of John and his civil war with the barons, how his army had made

England a land for the Devil, that indeed the Devil was to be found in every ditch and every corner of every field, an army which drew their swords and knives on all, ransacked towns, houses, cemeteries and churches, who tried to blot out everything, led by King John, that unnatural king. Isabella heard them, and heard the rhyme: with John's foul deeds England's whole realm was stinking, as Hell is too, where he is now sinking. She must make some grants or gifts for the salvation of his soul – three would be enough and all she could afford, or wanted to afford. Tithes of the Berkhamsted mills, a fair at Exeter for the monastery, something to the monks at Chichester so that they would say Masses for him. Letters written and sent; now she could put him out of her mind. She could think about herself and what to do next.

She walked the room, fretting and bitter, recounting grievances. 'The men who make up the regency say that a separate room shall be prepared for me at the castle in Exeter, that the present lodging is inadequate, but Eleanor's dower was promised to me when she died, not only Exeter but Wilton, Malmesbury, Ilchester – settlements which go back more than ten years and I still had to demand over and over again. But now at least I have a dower. By rights it should be one third of John's estate – not forthcoming. In truth my time in England has been one of dependence, humiliation and slander.'

Peter des Roches and Gualo requested a meeting. They knew they wanted no part of Isabella, a foreigner, a woman, and they both considered the task of being a valued member of the council beyond her. She had been too pert when young to learn how to hold her tongue, and was now too hasty.

'She has resources, quickly awarded, although Isabella does nothing but complain. I admit they are not magnificent, these dower lands, but she has more independence than ever before.'

'And what will she do? Set up a queen's court? This could be dangerous for such a time: she is untried, untested.'

'And what influence would she bring on the children? It has the potential to damage our careful plans to bring stability. Would she be prepared to return to France, a visit to her daughter there, perhaps? And she could govern Angoulême on the young king's behalf, keep it secure for him.'

The two men bowed and kissed hands. Isabella indicated chairs and they all three sat. A conference.

'We have thought about your requests for confirmation of your marriage portion, long outstanding.'

'And my interests are not only here in England but in France too: Saintes and Niort were given to me on my marriage day, the two richest lordships in Poitou. And I am the rightful heir to Angoulême as I have never forgotten, even though no one has made sure that my income from that county is in my treasury.'

'Indeed.'

The two men exchanged glances, and Gualo proceeded smoothly.

'As you know, the late king built up the navy to a considerable force. Hasten immediately, work night and day – those were his commands as he needed ships to sail around to La Rochelle when the Norman ports were lost to England.'

Isabella watched them, thoughtful. Where was this going?

'We know that there have been built some very well-appointed ships, not only for fighting but for trade and merchandise. We can confirm that one would be ready very easily if you wished to cross back to France.'

'With my pension promised and paid to me?' Isabella needed to be taken seriously by these two. She was conscious that her dignity had always been undermined by John. She had fought so hard to reclaim it, and now they would strip her of being queen mother, with a place in the politics of England.

Well, she had tried to initiate authority and it had not been appreciated. If she could at last gain what was hers, what had been promised in lands, tithes and a pension, she could return to Angoulême in triumph. And hadn't she planned to do this for herself, thought about this choice very recently? And now she was being offered a fine ship and sincere promises of her income.

'With your rights restored, confirmed, no limits on your endowments.'

It was swiftly agreed and Isabella set to, packing up the silks and linens and furs, ells of material. She folded silk twill, cambric; wrapped a mirror that had once been mended after she threw it at John and he had thrown it back at her, cracking it against the fireplace. The two gold cups he had given her after the births of Henry and Richard. Last, she took her seals, the great seal and the smaller, more personal one; these were important emblems of her standing, and she would use them always. They were carefully parcelled into a red wool bag lined with blue linen; a beautiful bag appliqued with vines, the scrolling foliage and silky tassels stitched so carefully. She raised it to her lips and then placed it in the small, iron-bound chest, made all those years ago in Angoulême.

De Mauley brought Richard to Winchester and there she said goodbye to her four children, Henry still and grave-faced, learning to be a king; Richard fidgeting with a small wooden sword, learning to be a soldier.

'They call me Henry of Winchester, Mother, because I was born here and it is a holy place.'

'He cries when we have sermons.' Richard was not sure if this was a good thing or not.

'I am sure you are both upright, honest, loving boys. Soon to be young men.'

Isabella kissed them and quickly picked up Eleanor and

Isabelle, first one, then the other. They squirmed and fussed as she whispered goodbye. She put them down, and briskly turned away.

The ship was waiting in Dover, that town which was the key to England, and calm in the mid-July sunshine, a tranquil sea outside the harbour. It was indeed a well-appointed ship, with all the respect and honour possible provided for a queen. A ship that would take her to where she had power and influence.

Peter des Roches stood by her as they watched the ship being loaded with the last of her stoutly bound trunks. He wondered a little what she would do now: she had left her sons in England, that had to be, for one was king and one was the heir to the throne, but what of her daughters? So young to leave behind, but Isabella did not seem distressed by their parting, and neither did she talk of longing to see Joan again. She was pleased to be leaving this country, he thought; more than pleased – eager, and taking the earliest possible opportunity. The offer of the ship was a good bribe but he suspected she would have left without it, carelessly, almost happily, abandoning her four children by John.

She turned to him as the time came to board. 'Goodbye, Peter des Roches. We both remember when you were Archdeacon of Poitiers. Now you are guardian to a king, my son, and Bishop of Winchester, rich and powerful. I hope you will remain so for the sake of Henry. The English like less and less the men who have ties to France.'

He bowed over her outstretched hand and said, 'And you will be back in the country south of the Loire, where the lords and counts do not care for the kings of France or England, as well I know.'

Isabella smiled, 'As a proud Poitevin I chime with that: we have no need for royalty. Angoulême and its domains need me now – there is much to do and I intend to take possession of my territory with some speed, and be someone who commands, as Countess of Angoulême and Dowager Queen of England.'

Des Roches bit back any cutting remark, for Isabella was embarking and he merely wished her a safe voyage and Godspeed, raising his arm in blessing as she walked up to the ship where Terric waited for her, a brave soldier and the only man to have won her trust. He had escorted Isabella and guarded her, and kept her safe through the civil war. He had no need to be in England anymore, and was gladly taking her back to Angoulême.

I hope I can use this time well, she thought as she watched the chalky cliffs disappear. A long voyage would give time to think, to reflect, perhaps to dwell hard and long on past indignities and offences against her person. And to plan a future where she was powerful.

The ride from La Rochelle took the road from the coast south to Pons, the gateway town; the flat plain clearly marked by the castle and hospital for abandoned children. The streets thronged with the poor and the pilgrims making their way to Spain and St James' shrine. A good place to stop for the night before they rode on past Cognac, south of Poitiers, south of Lusignan. Joan was there with her Lusignan fiancé. Isabella imagined her daughter's life to be much as hers had been: sewing, embroidery, arithmetic, weaving and listening to the women's stories. She would soon be able to visit and talk to her and Hugh le Brun, last seen seventeen years ago, a boy intent only on hunting when Isabella rode away with her father to be married to John.

Hugh had been kind and she remembered him as young, quiet, watchful, doing his father's bidding without discord. He would suit Joan, who had no rebellion in her. And his father, the knight who had been betrothed to Isabella and who had expected to marry her after all those solemn vows were made, she had heard last year that he had gone on a crusade, perhaps leaving his wife, her cousin Mathilde, in Lusignan. There might be land titles to discuss now I am home, Isabella thought. An easy visit to make, to see them all in Lusignan, when everything was settled in Angoulême. She should try to visit her mother too, living north of here, close to Paris, not so easy, a long ride from Angoulême.

Her mother had governed the city for a few months after Ademar's death, and John had given her a pension, all paid out of the Norman exchequer, the generous rich treasury of Normandy. Well, that had all collapsed, thought Isabella, and many people suffered when it dried up. But it had helped her mother for some time and then she had been happy to retire to Champagne. An inheritance from her first husband, the Count of Joigny, Alice was lucky to have a place to go to. But Philippe had not trusted her and she'd been made to swear not to make any kind of treaty or alliance with John. He'd demanded a pledge of 2,000 silver marks, to make sure she kept her word and the de Courtney family had found the money for her. Such a well-connected family; it was worth remembering that.

But soon enough, Isabella told herself, to follow family matters, she must make for Angoulême.

There would be nobody close to her there: but it was good to think that soon she could have her own people around her, denied for so long: no body of kinsmen and no servants from home to go with her to London. No wonder she had been so pleased to see Peter when he arrived at the English court. And he had fought on John's side too, against Philippe, so he had been a loyal half-brother. She shook her head as if to shake away the dreadful rumours of incest that had been so damaging to her reputation.

Angoulême could be seen now, the castle high on the hill

above the river, always an important place, holding a strong vantage point. Granted a mayor and commune and freedom from customs, John had been careful to keep the citizens on his side. The mayor had been appointed just two days before Isabella's father died.

Bartholomew de la Puy – she had met him when last here in 1214, when the disastrous Battle of Bouvines had been fought further north. He had welcomed her and served her chines of venison, an acknowledgement of her standing.

There was a new mayor now, d'Aurifont, and here he was, beaming, enthusiastic and Isabella received the keys of the city for him. It was a triumph for the Countess of Angoulême, home at last to the castle on the hill, hers to keep and to hold.

Acknowledgements

Thanks to Philippa Pride for running an excellent workshop in south-west France in 2011, which kick-started the whole process of creative writing. Thanks to Stephen Carver, the tutor for the online writing course at UEA, and thanks for Judith Laverty, Colin Hodson and Kate Cartwright, who were virtual course members and then became writing friends, always encouraging, clear-eyed and supportive. Thanks to Dan Bessie and all the members of the Every Other Friday writing group in Mareuil because they made me focus and keep on writing. Thanks to Biggles, who always told me when it was time to stop writing and go for a walk.

Thanks to John, generous in giving me time and space, then, now and always.